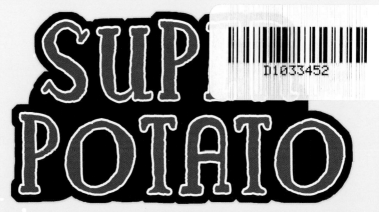

SUPER POTATO

#4 SUPER POTATO AND THE MUTANT ANIMAL MAYHEM

ARTUR LAPERLA

Graphic Universe™ • Minneapolis

Story and illustrations by Artur Laperla
Translation by Norwyn MacTíre

First American edition published in 2020 by Graphic Universe™

Copyright © 2015 by Artur Laperla and Bang. Ediciones. Published by arrangement with
Garbuix Agency.

Graphic Universe™ is a trademark of Lerner Publishing Group, Inc.

Graphic Universe™
An imprint of Lerner Publishing Group, Inc.
241 First Avenue North
Minneapolis, MN 55401 USA

For reading levels and more information, look up this title at www.lernerbooks.com.

Main body text set in CCWildWords. Typeface provided by Comicraft.

Library of Congress Cataloging-in-Publication Data

Names: Laperla (Artist) author, illustrator. | MacTíre, Norwyn, translator.
Title: Super Potato and the mutant animal mayhem / story and illustrations by Artur
    Laperla ; translation by Norwyn MacTíre.
Other titles: Venganza de Malicia la Maligna. English
Description: First American edition. | Minneapolis : Graphic Universe, 2020. | Series: Super
    Potato ; book 4 | Summary: "An enemy linked to Super Potato's past sets a trap for the
    hero in the form of a giant chicken" —Provided by publisher.
Identifiers: LCCN 2019008575 | ISBN 9781512440249 (lb : alk. paper)
Subjects: LCSH: Graphic novels. | CYAC: Graphic novels. | Superheroes—Fiction. | Potatoes—
    Fiction. | Humorous stories.
Classification: LCC PZ7.7.L367 Sr 2020 | DDC 741.5/973—dc23

LC record available at https://lccn.loc.gov/2019008575

Manufactured in the United States of America
1-42293-26143-5/29/2019

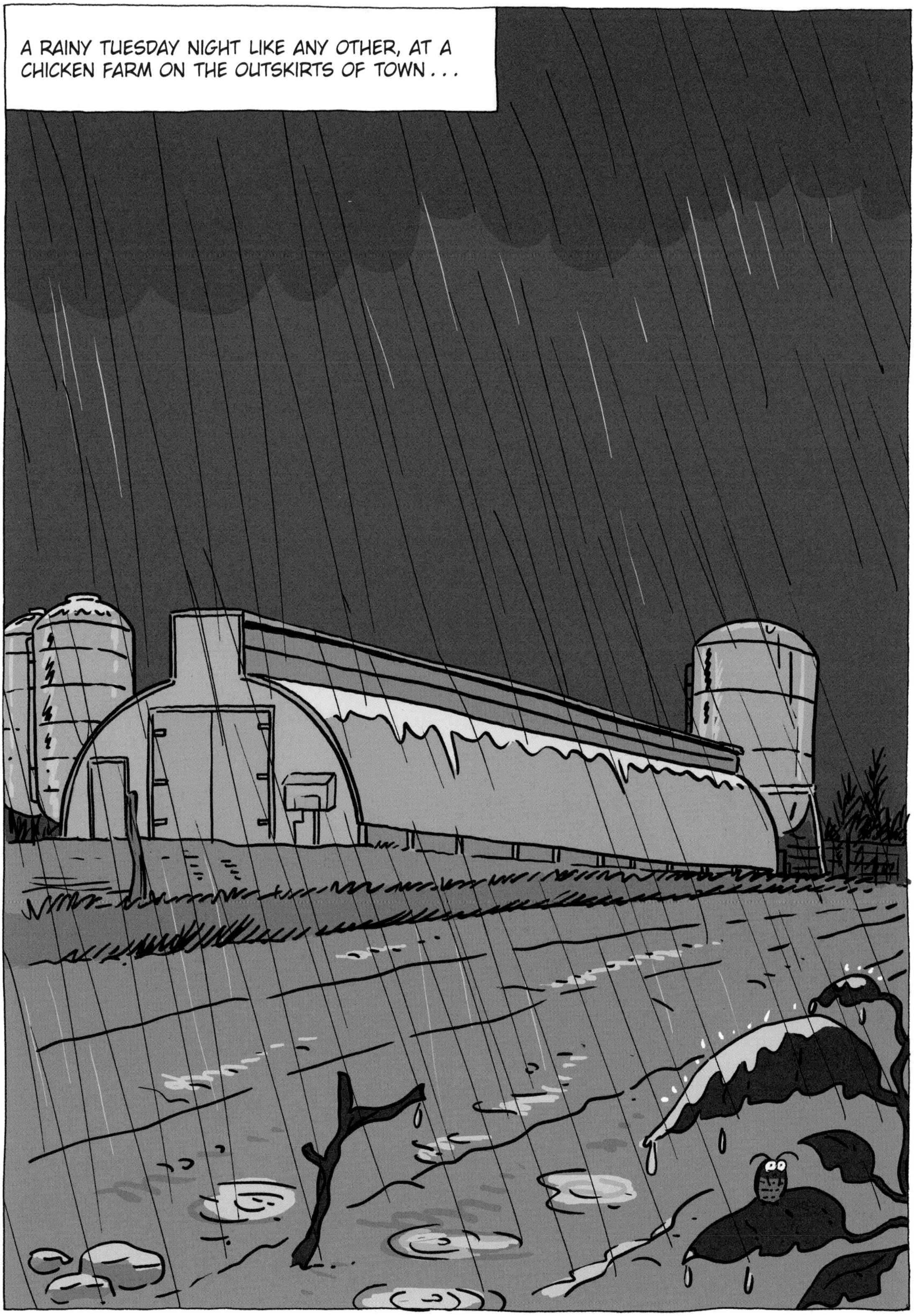
A RAINY TUESDAY NIGHT LIKE ANY OTHER, AT A CHICKEN FARM ON THE OUTSKIRTS OF TOWN . . .

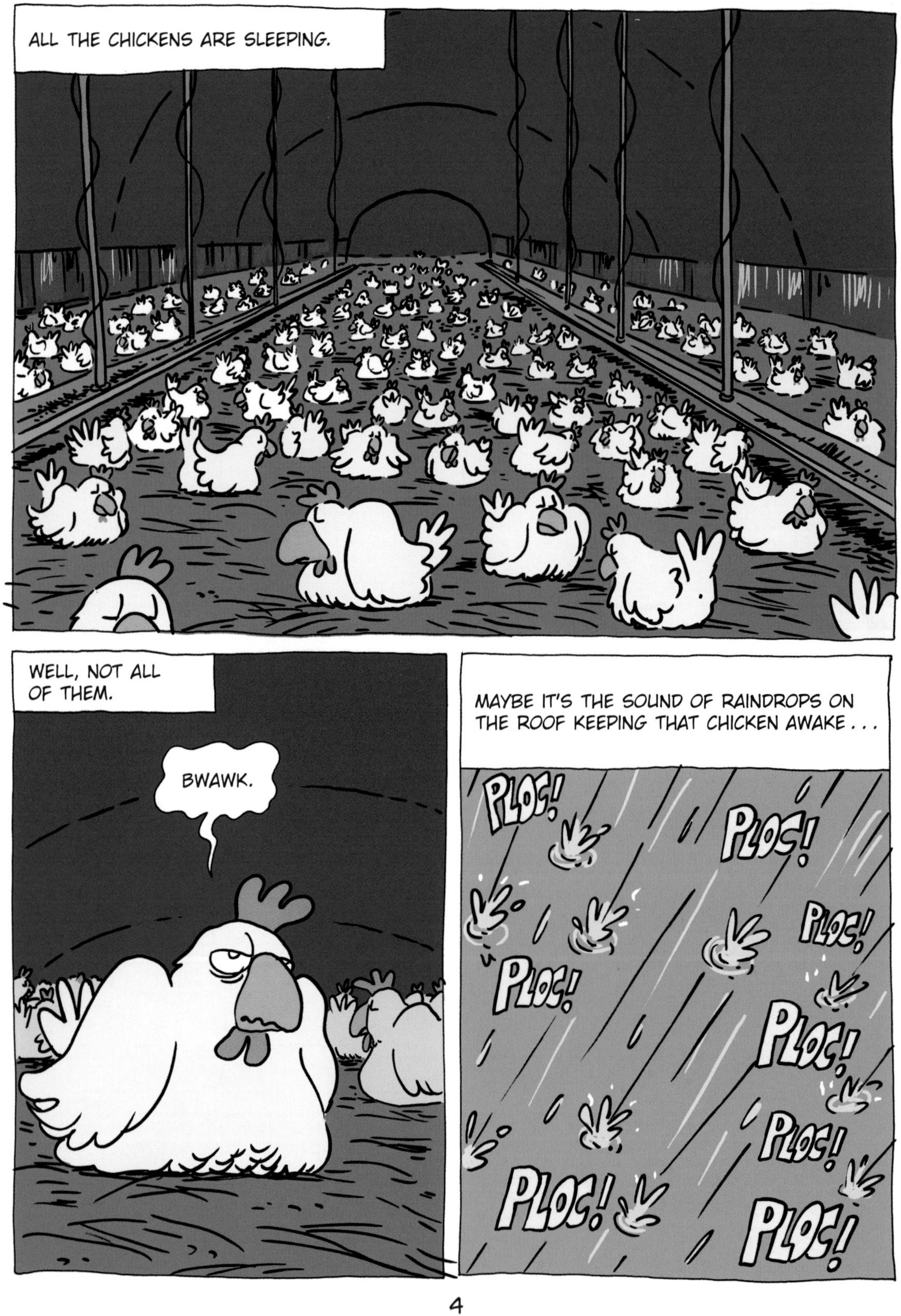
ALL THE CHICKENS ARE SLEEPING.
WELL, NOT ALL OF THEM.
BWAWK.
MAYBE IT'S THE SOUND OF RAINDROPS ON THE ROOF KEEPING THAT CHICKEN AWAKE . . .
PLOC!
PLOC!
PLOC!
PLOC!
PLOC!
PLOC!
PLOC!
PLOC!

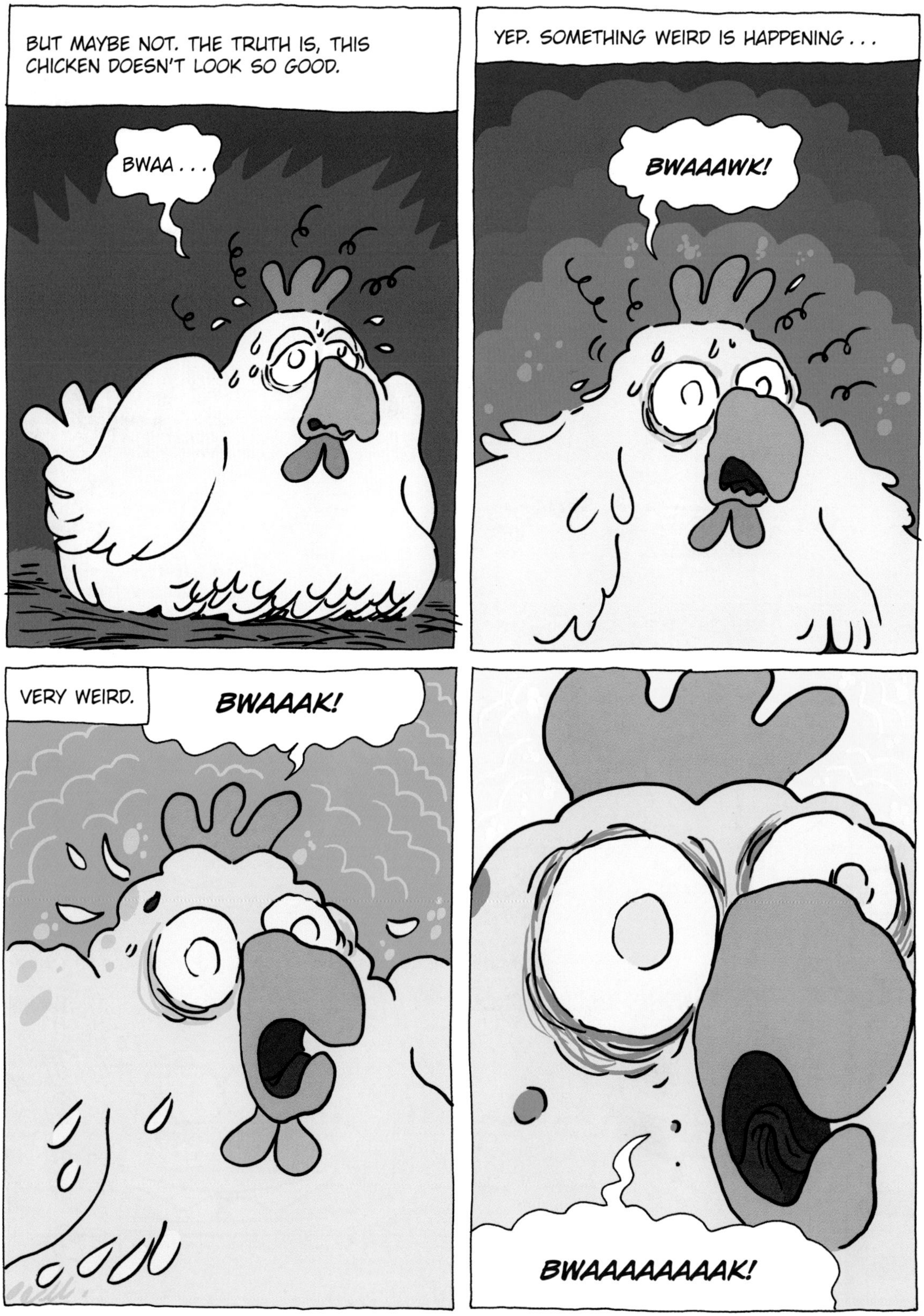
BUT MAYBE NOT. THE TRUTH IS, THIS CHICKEN DOESN'T LOOK SO GOOD.
BWAA . . .
YEP. SOMETHING WEIRD IS HAPPENING . . .
BWAAAWK!
VERY WEIRD.
BWAAAK!
BWAAAAAAAAK!

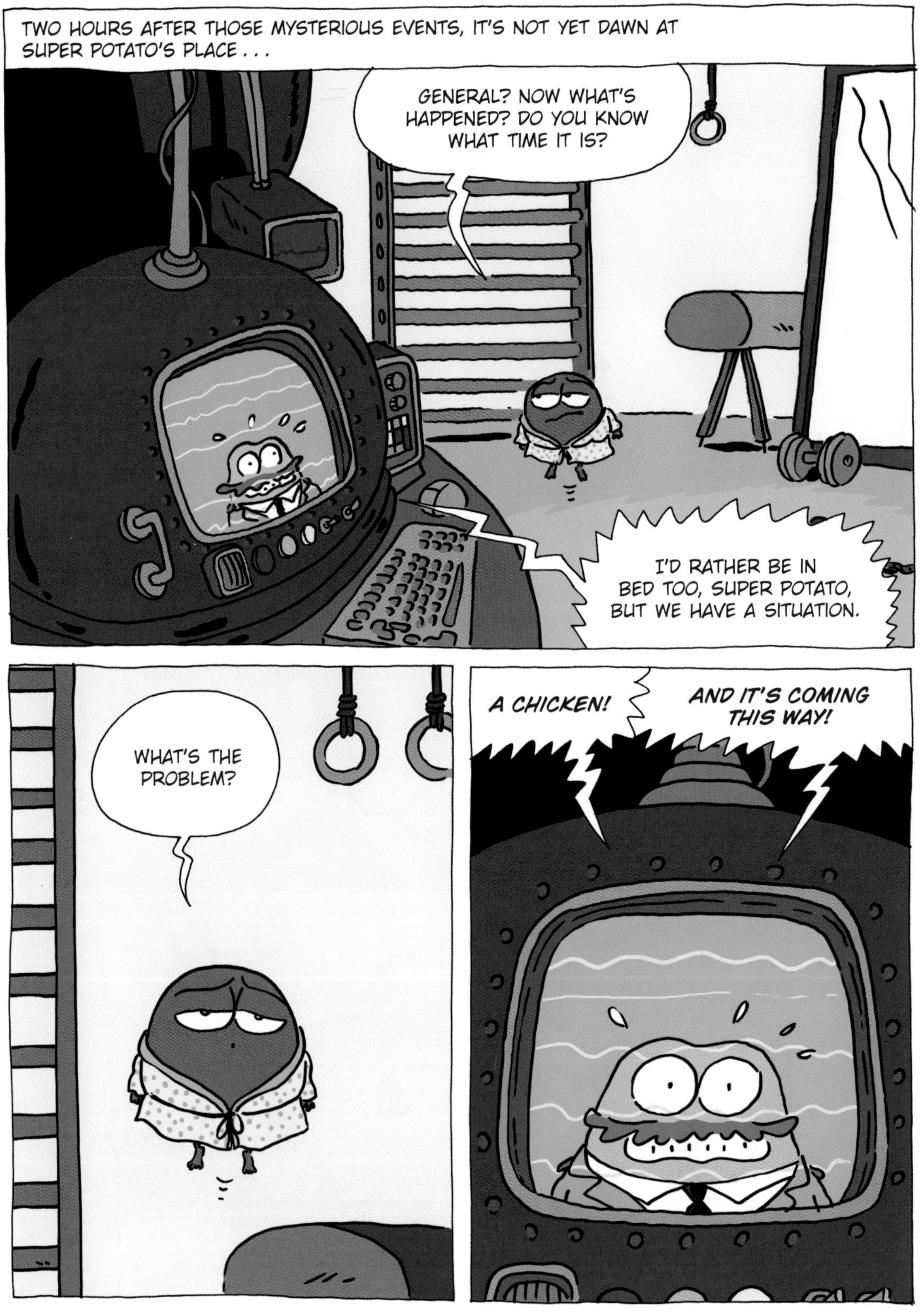
TWO HOURS AFTER THOSE MYSTERIOUS EVENTS, IT'S NOT YET DAWN AT SUPER POTATO'S PLACE . . .
GENERAL? NOW WHAT'S HAPPENED? DO YOU KNOW WHAT TIME IT IS?
I'D RATHER BE IN BED TOO, SUPER POTATO, BUT WE HAVE A SITUATION.
WHAT'S THE PROBLEM?
A CHICKEN!
AND IT'S COMING THIS WAY!

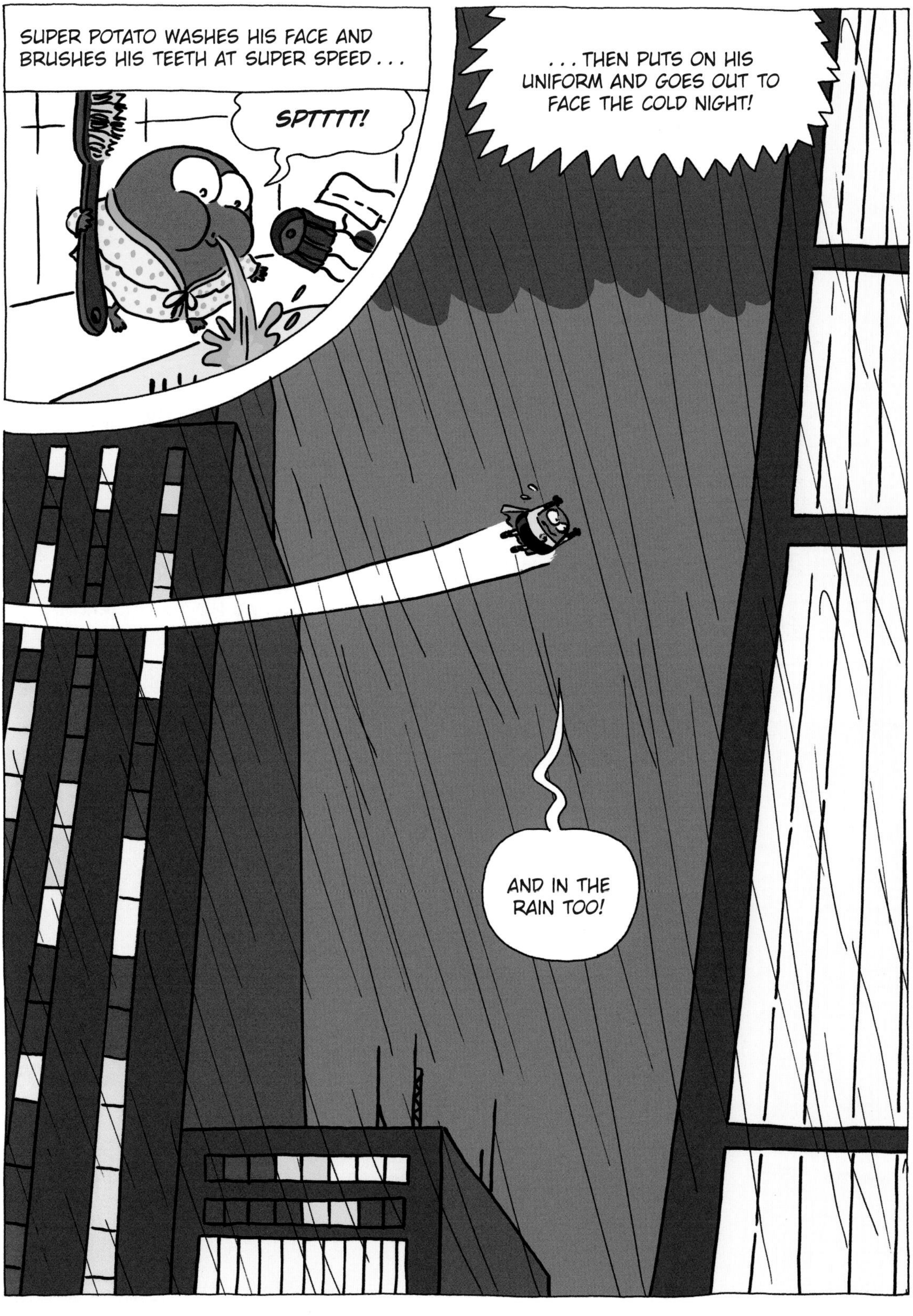
SUPER POTATO WASHES HIS FACE AND BRUSHES HIS TEETH AT SUPER SPEED . . .
SPTTTT!
. . . THEN PUTS ON HIS UNIFORM AND GOES OUT TO FACE THE COLD NIGHT!
AND IN THE RAIN TOO!

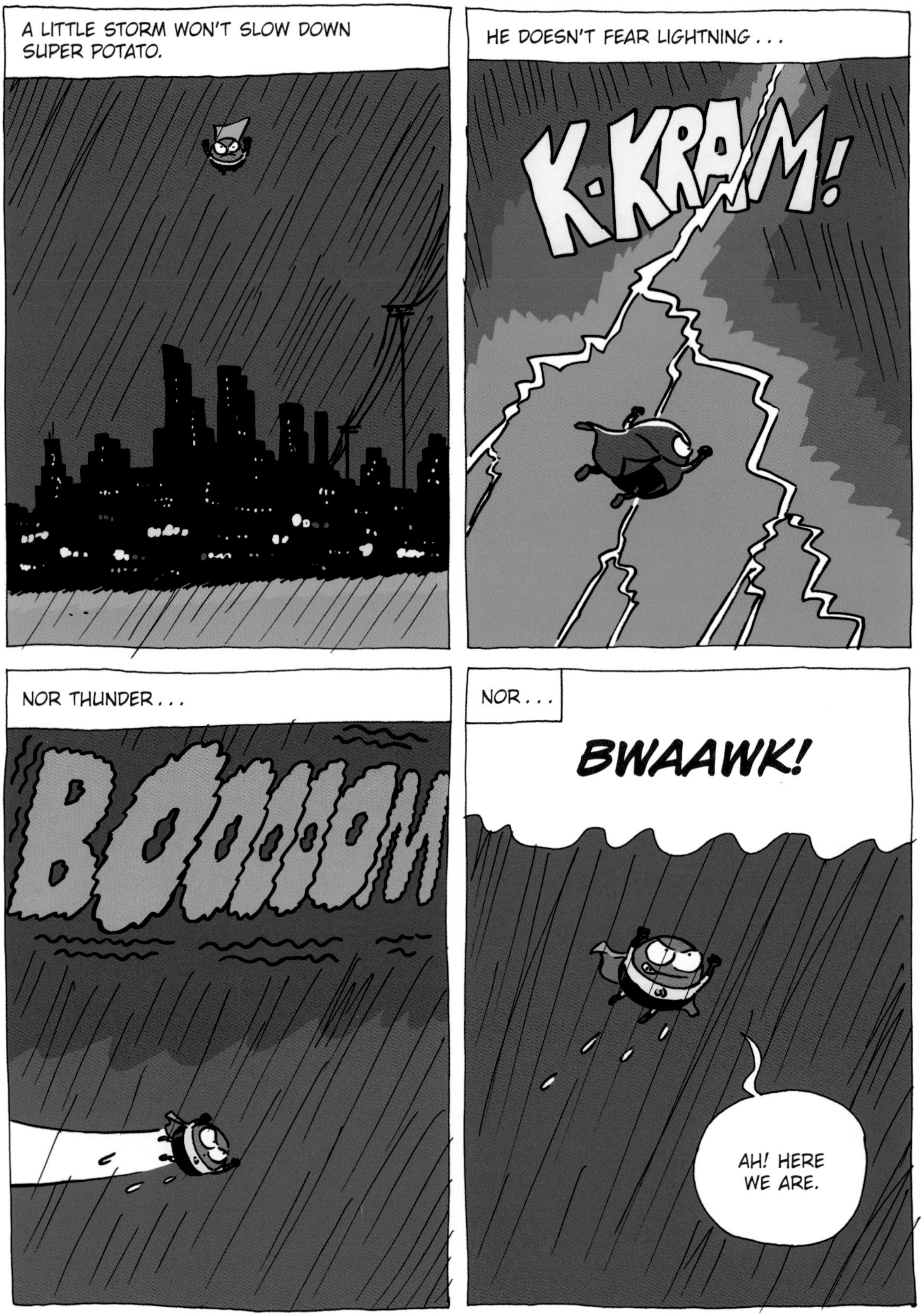
A LITTLE STORM WON'T SLOW DOWN SUPER POTATO.
HE DOESN'T FEAR LIGHTNING . . .
K-KRAM!
NOR THUNDER . . .
BOOOOM
NOR . . .
BWAAWK!
AH! HERE WE ARE.

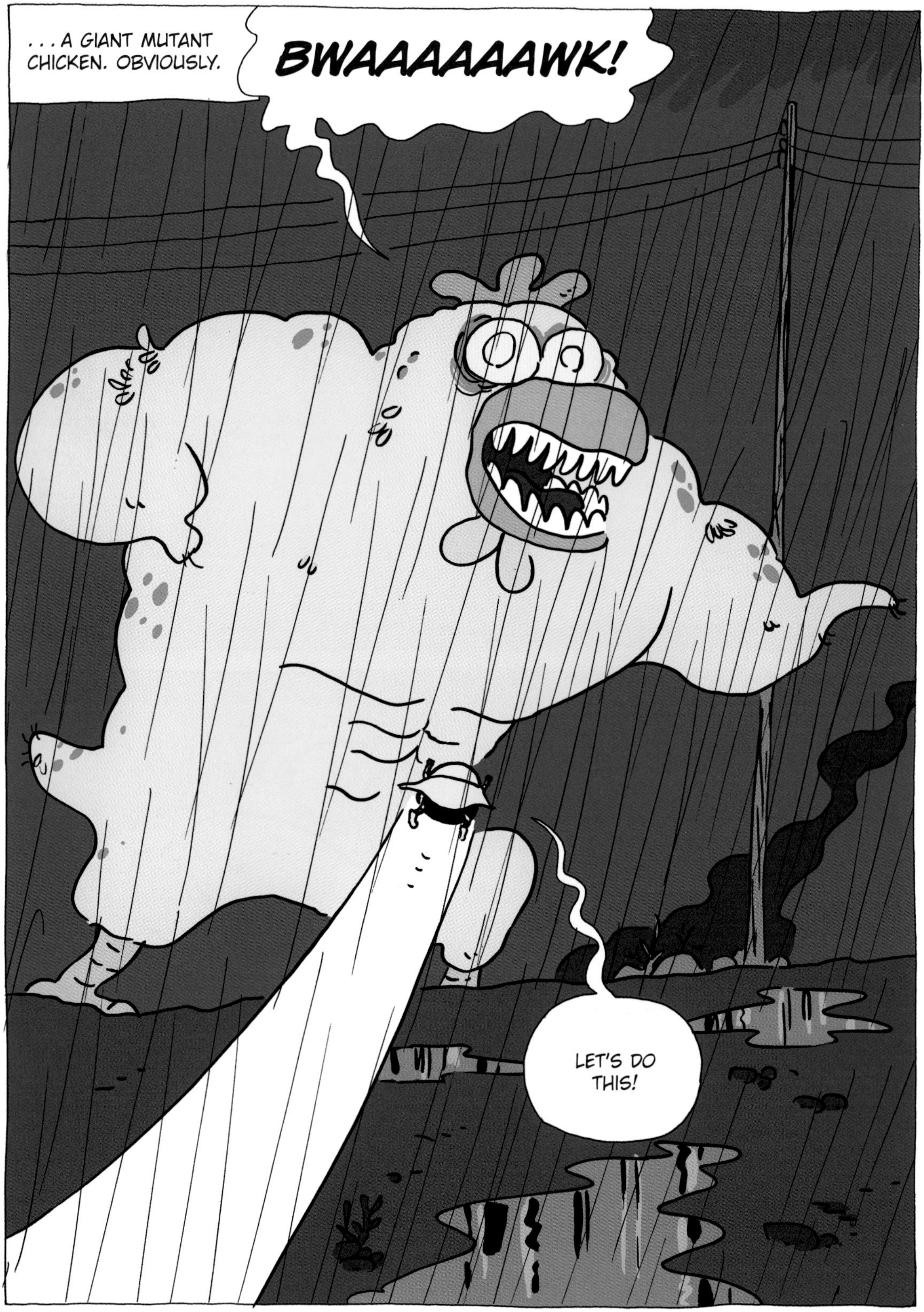

. . . A GIANT MUTANT CHICKEN. OBVIOUSLY.
BWAAAAAAAWK!
LET'S DO THIS!

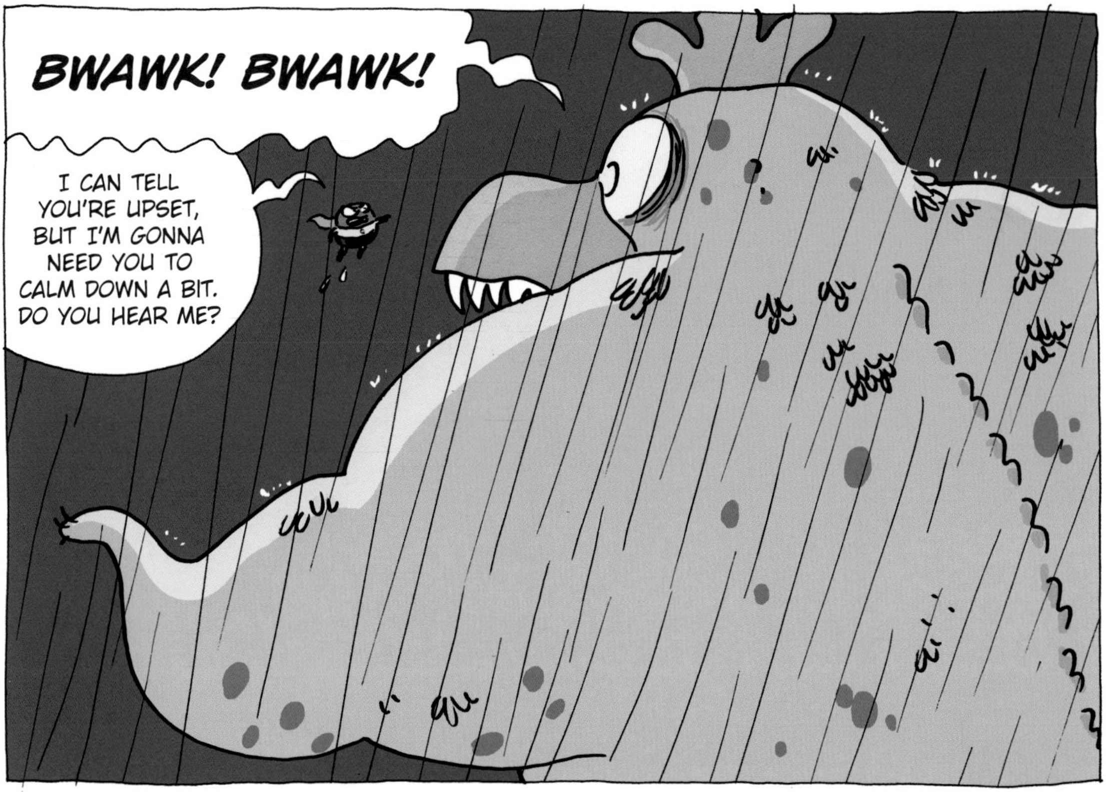
BWAWK! BWAWK!
I CAN TELL YOU'RE UPSET, BUT I'M GONNA NEED YOU TO CALM DOWN A BIT. DO YOU HEAR ME?

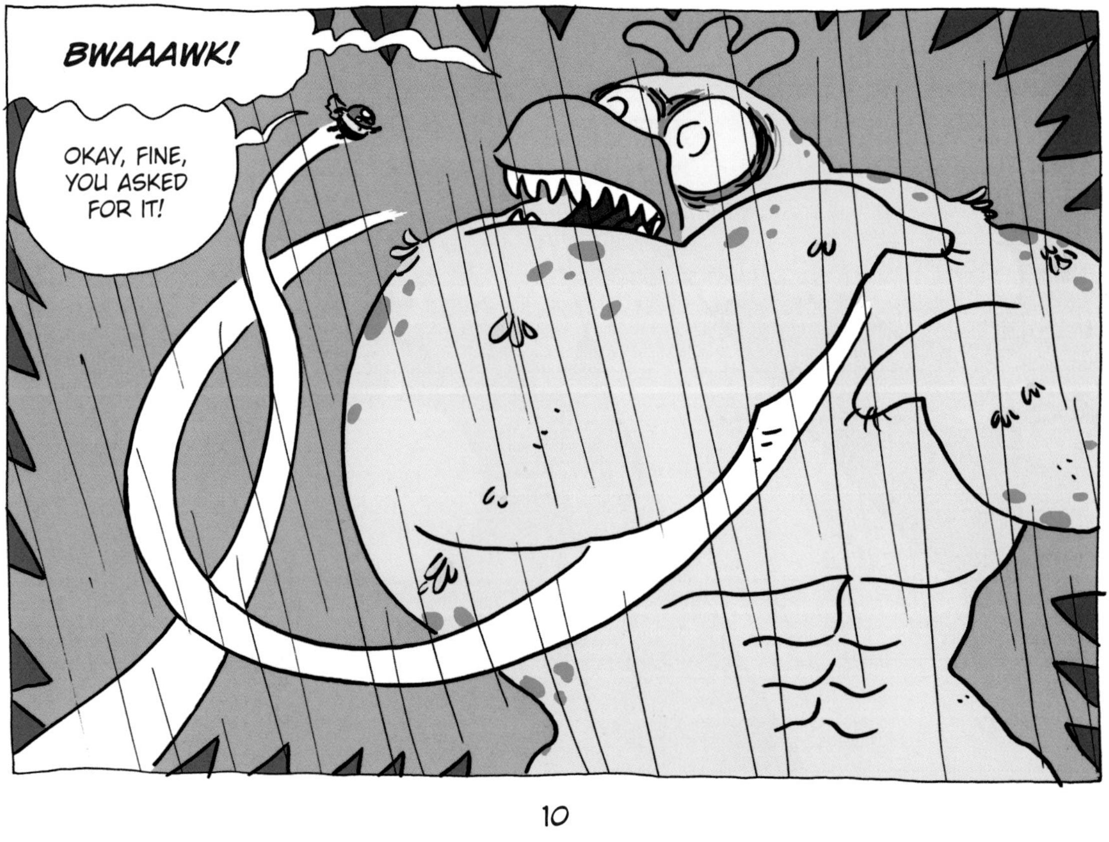
BWAAAWK!
OKAY, FINE, YOU ASKED FOR IT!

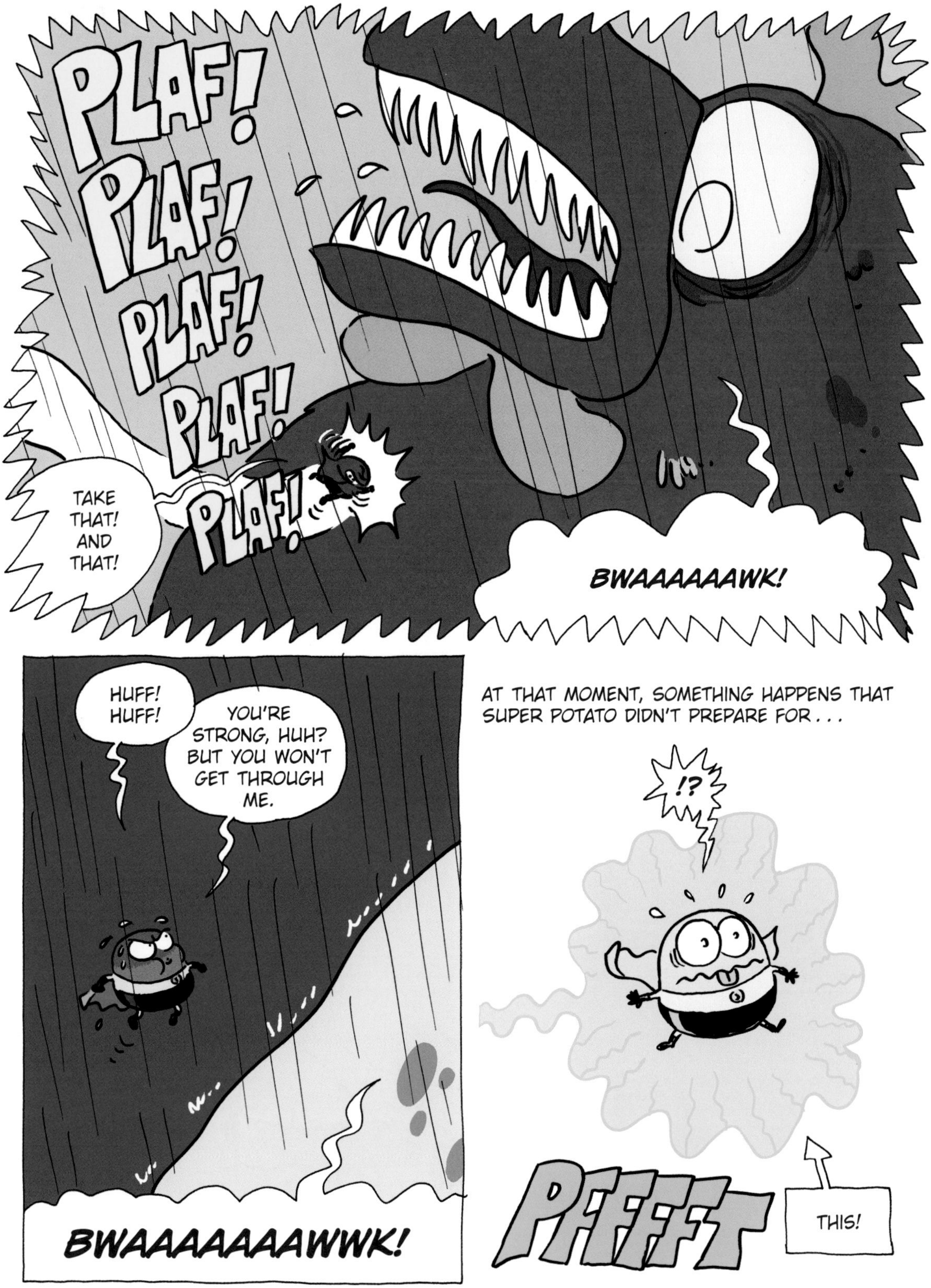
PLAF!
PLAF!
PLAF!
PLAF!
PLAF!
TAKE THAT! AND THAT!
BWAAAAAAWK!
HUFF! HUFF!
YOU'RE STRONG, HUH? BUT YOU WON'T GET THROUGH ME.
BWAAAAAAAAWWK!
AT THAT MOMENT, SOMETHING HAPPENS THAT SUPER POTATO DIDN'T PREPARE FOR . . .
!?
PFFFFT
THIS!

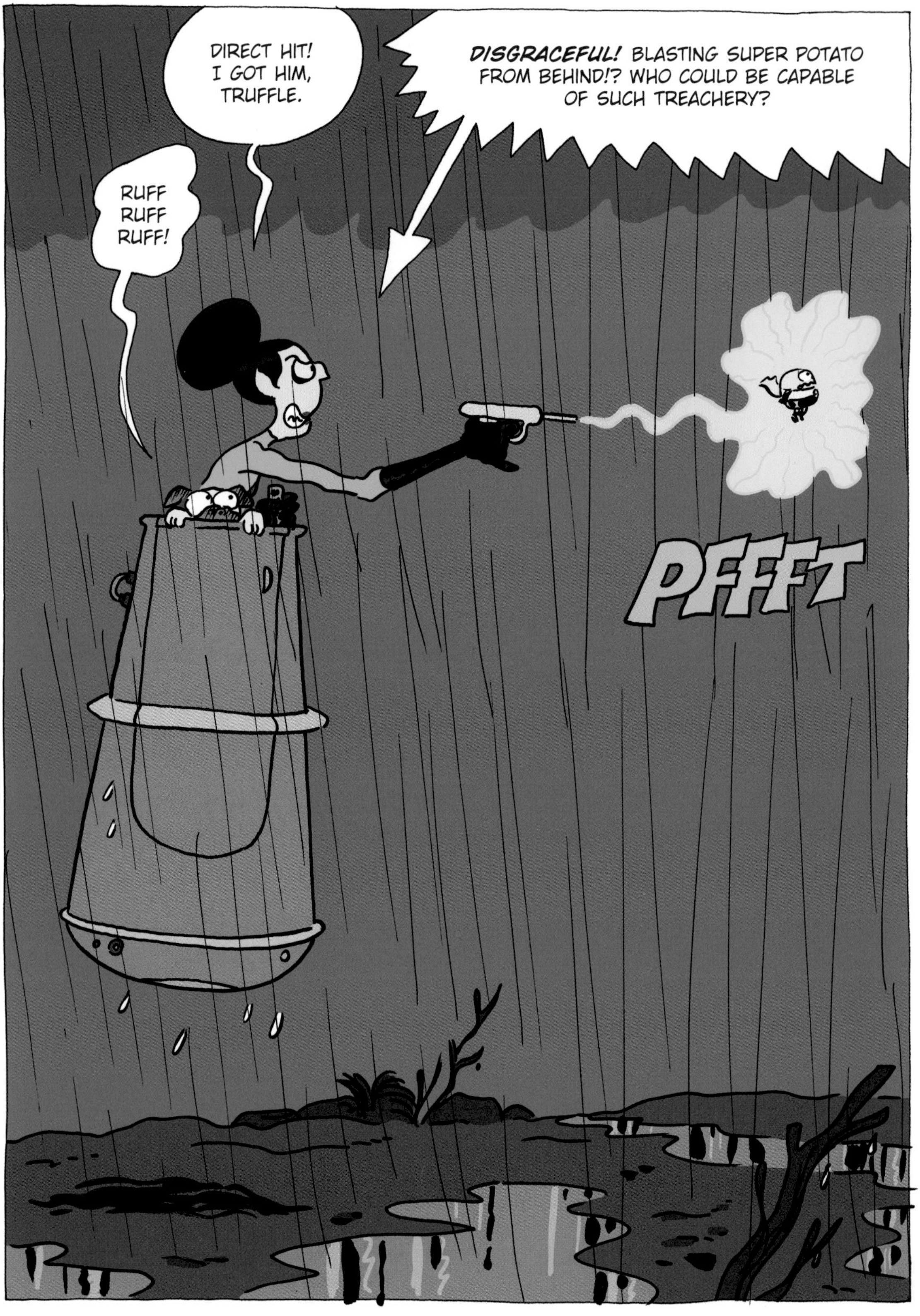
RUFF RUFF RUFF!
DIRECT HIT! I GOT HIM, TRUFFLE.
DISGRACEFUL! BLASTING SUPER POTATO FROM BEHIND!? WHO COULD BE CAPABLE OF SUCH TREACHERY?
PFFFT

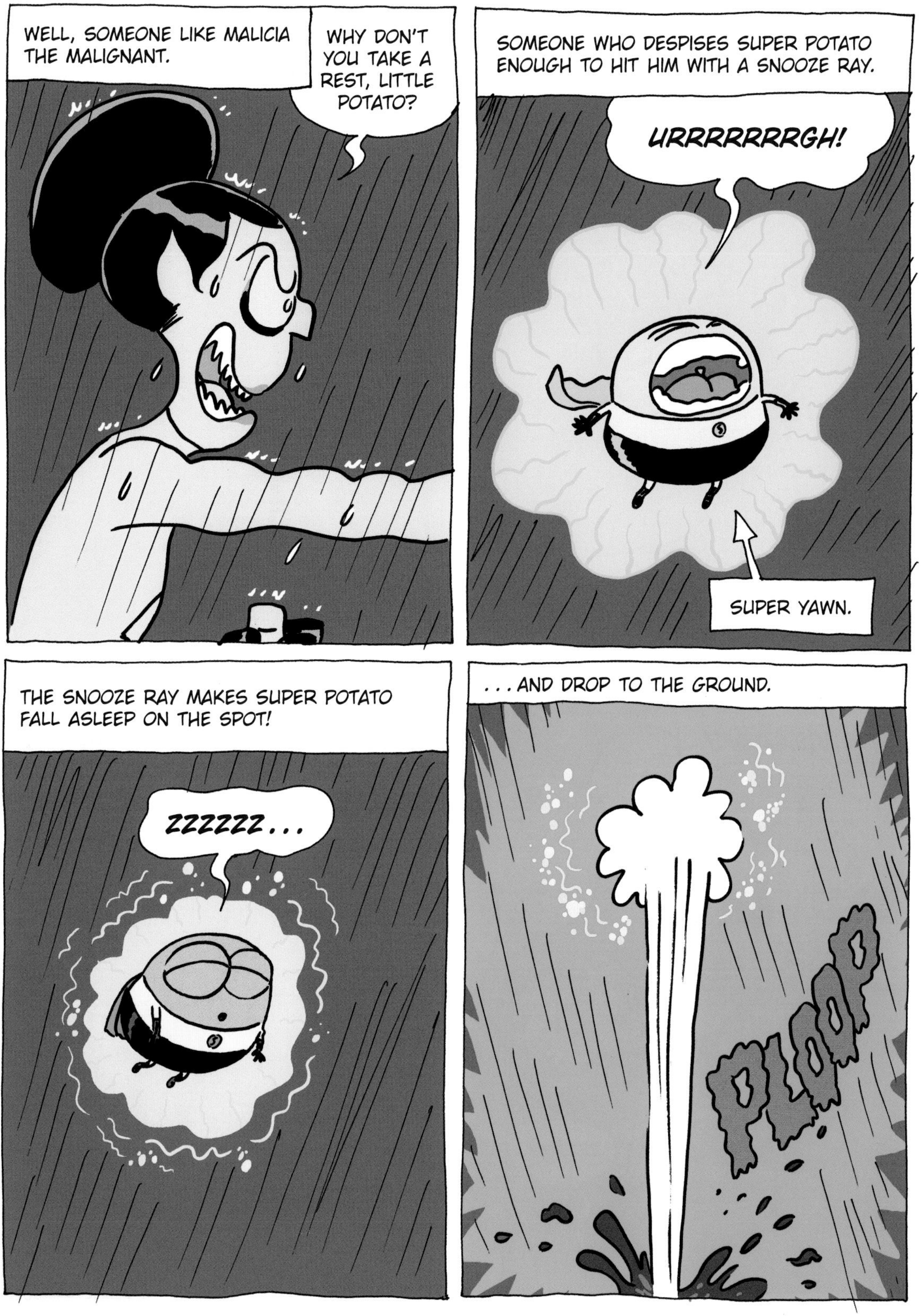
WELL, SOMEONE LIKE MALICIA THE MALIGNANT.
WHY DON'T YOU TAKE A REST, LITTLE POTATO?
SOMEONE WHO DESPISES SUPER POTATO ENOUGH TO HIT HIM WITH A SNOOZE RAY.
URRRRRRRGH!
SUPER YAWN.
THE SNOOZE RAY MAKES SUPER POTATO FALL ASLEEP ON THE SPOT!
ZZZZZZ . . .
. . . AND DROP TO THE GROUND.
PLOOP

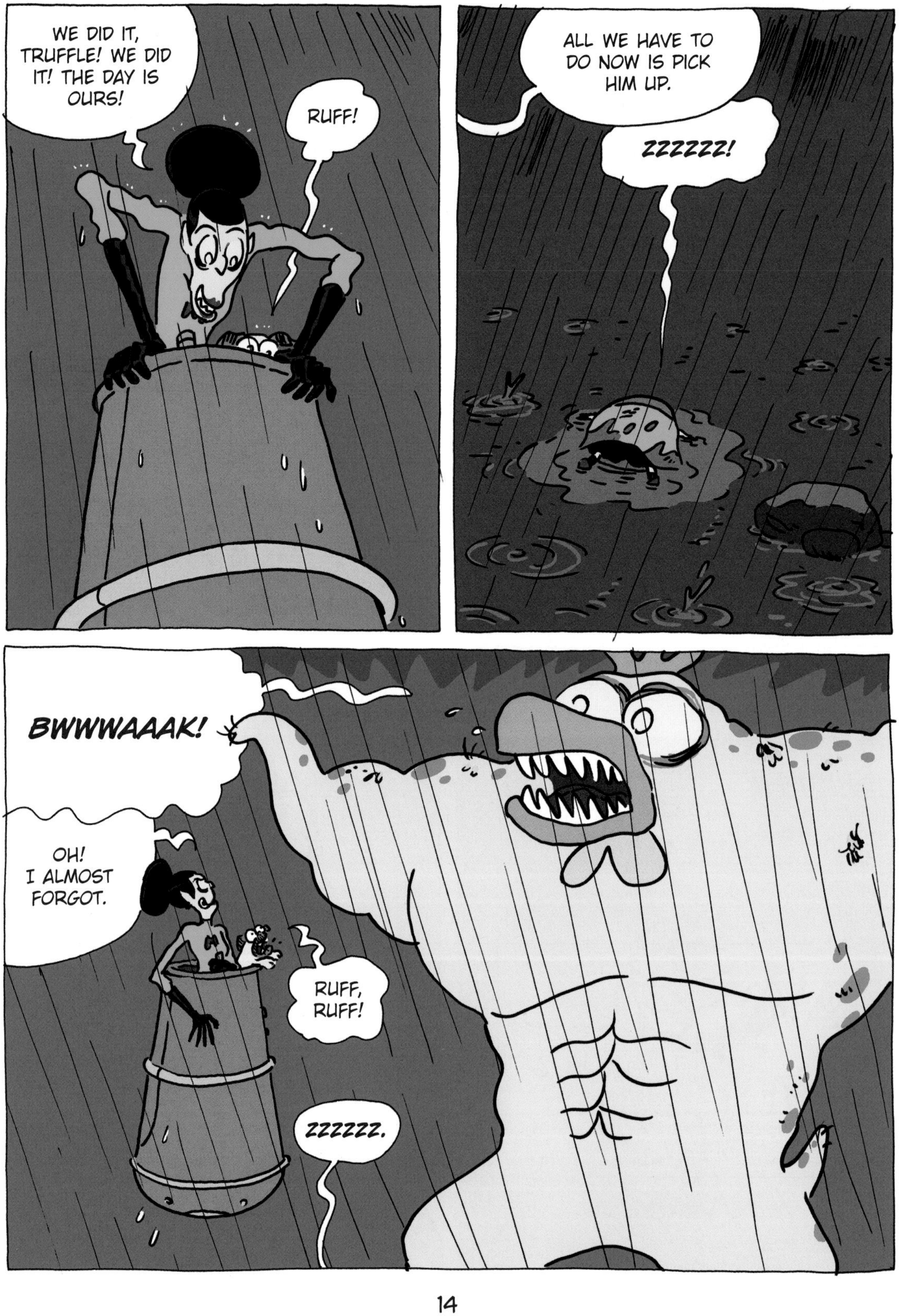
WE DID IT, TRUFFLE! WE DID IT! THE DAY IS OURS!
RUFF!
ALL WE HAVE TO DO NOW IS PICK HIM UP.
ZZZZZZ!
BWWWAAAK!
OH! I ALMOST FORGOT.
RUFF, RUFF!
ZZZZZZ.

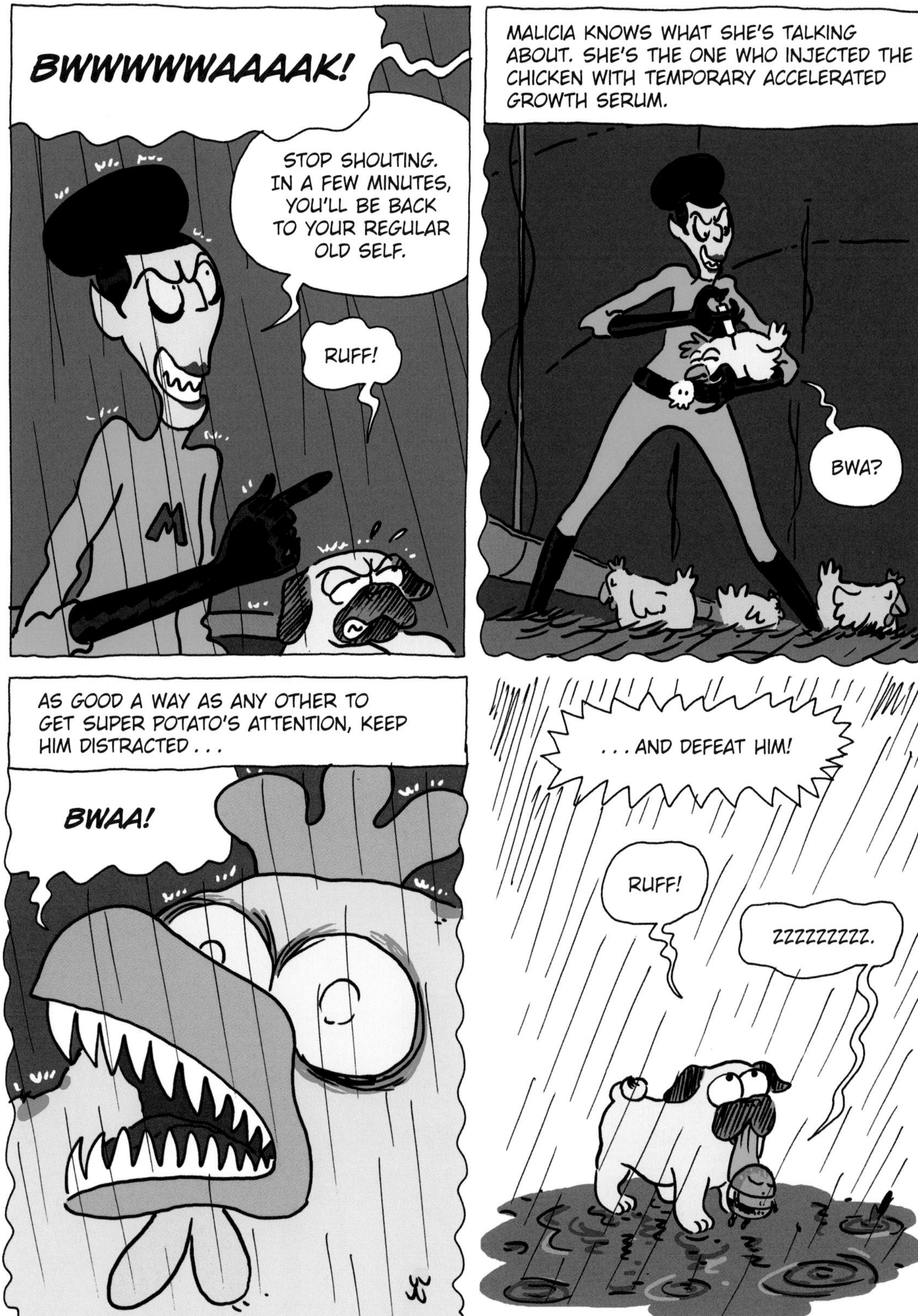
BWWWWWAAAAK!
STOP SHOUTING. IN A FEW MINUTES, YOU'LL BE BACK TO YOUR REGULAR OLD SELF.
RUFF!
MALICIA KNOWS WHAT SHE'S TALKING ABOUT. SHE'S THE ONE WHO INJECTED THE CHICKEN WITH TEMPORARY ACCELERATED GROWTH SERUM.
BWA?
AS GOOD A WAY AS ANY OTHER TO GET SUPER POTATO'S ATTENTION, KEEP HIM DISTRACTED . . .
BWAA!
. . . AND DEFEAT HIM!
RUFF!
ZZZZZZZZZ.

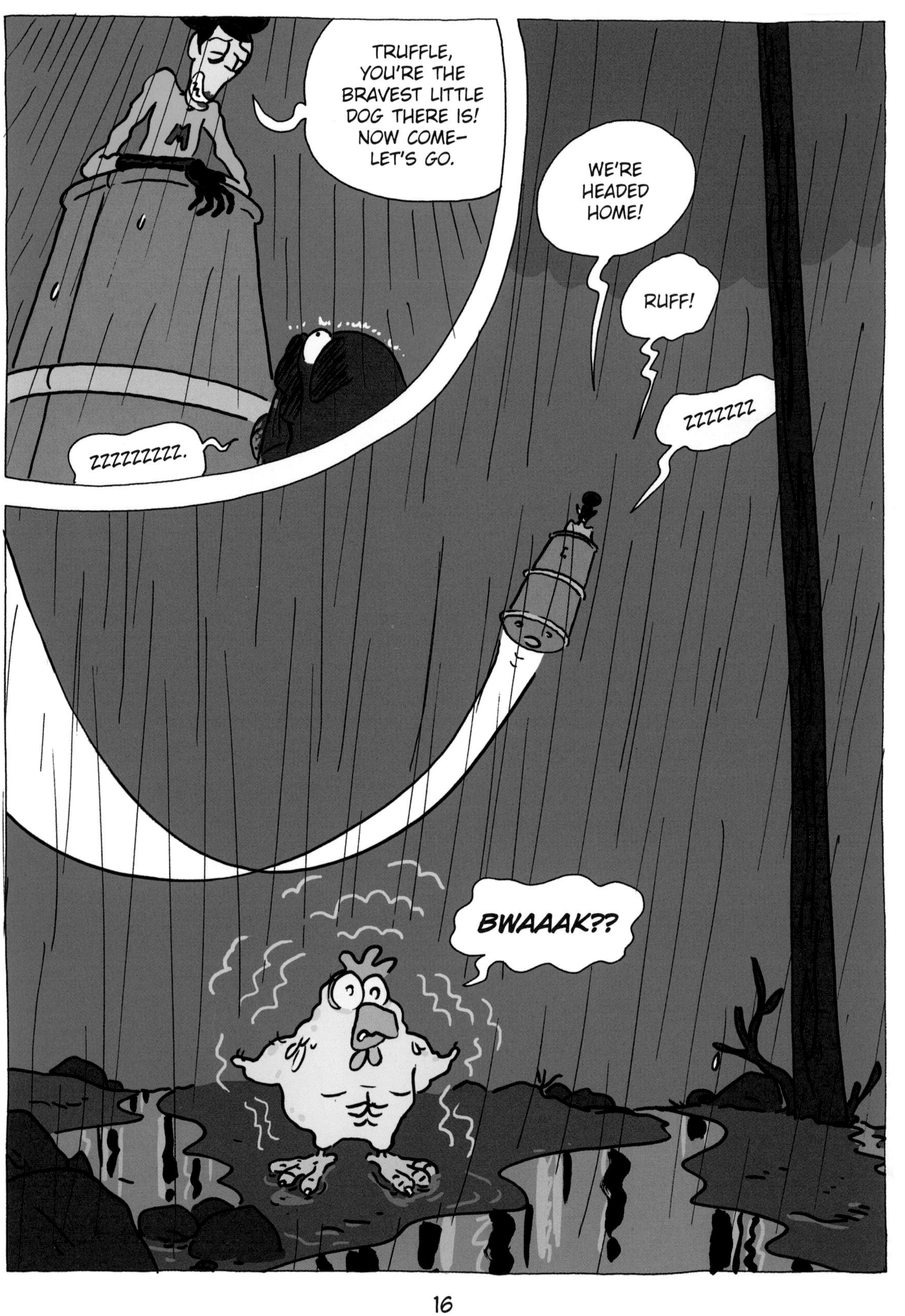
TRUFFLE, YOU'RE THE BRAVEST LITTLE DOG THERE IS! NOW COME– LET'S GO.
ZZZZZZZZZ.
WE'RE HEADED HOME!
RUFF!
ZZZZZZZ
BWAAAK??

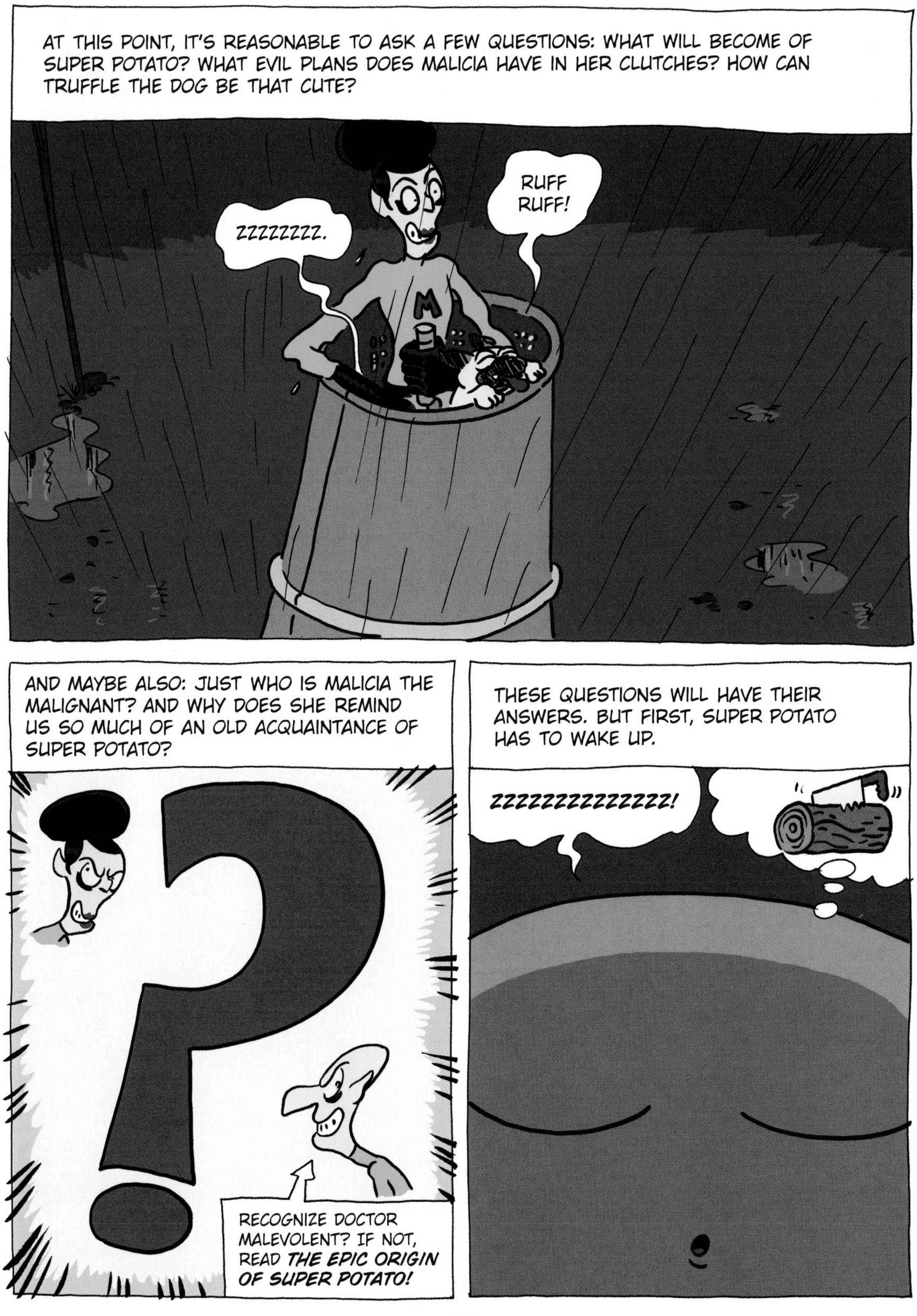
AT THIS POINT, IT'S REASONABLE TO ASK A FEW QUESTIONS: WHAT WILL BECOME OF SUPER POTATO? WHAT EVIL PLANS DOES MALICIA HAVE IN HER CLUTCHES? HOW CAN TRUFFLE THE DOG BE THAT CUTE?
ZZZZZZZZ.
RUFF RUFF!
AND MAYBE ALSO: JUST WHO IS MALICIA THE MALIGNANT? AND WHY DOES SHE REMIND US SO MUCH OF AN OLD ACQUAINTANCE OF SUPER POTATO?
RECOGNIZE DOCTOR MALEVOLENT? IF NOT, READ ***THE EPIC ORIGIN OF SUPER POTATO!***
THESE QUESTIONS WILL HAVE THEIR ANSWERS. BUT FIRST, SUPER POTATO HAS TO WAKE UP.
ZZZZZZZZZZZZZZZ!

EXACTLY EIGHT HOURS AFTER FALLING ASLEEP...

MMMH...

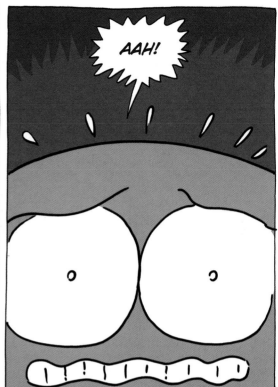

AAH!

WHAT THE!?

GRRRRRRRR!

18

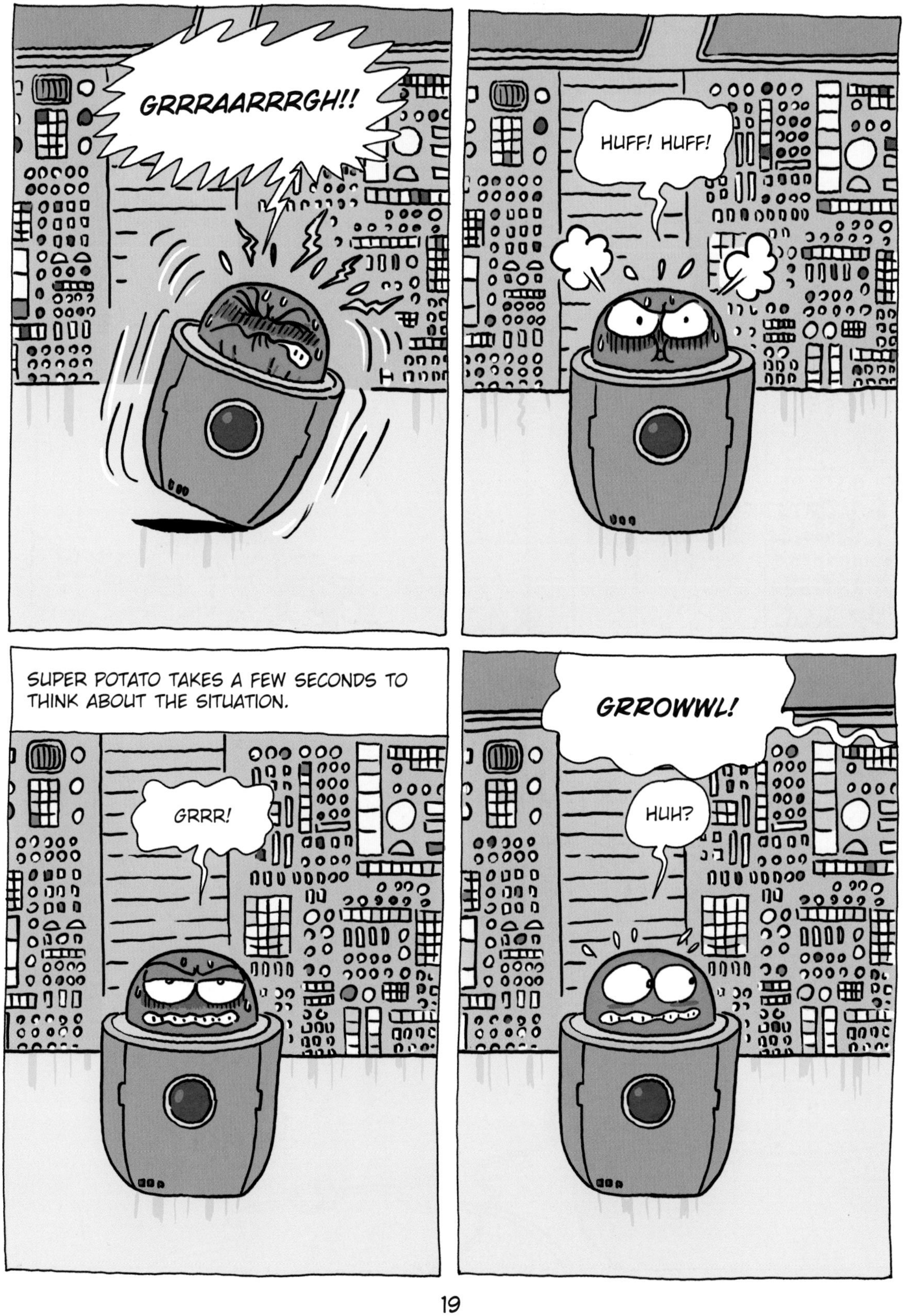
GRRRAARRRGH!!
HUFF! HUFF!
SUPER POTATO TAKES A FEW SECONDS TO THINK ABOUT THE SITUATION.
GRRR!
GRROWWL!
HUH?

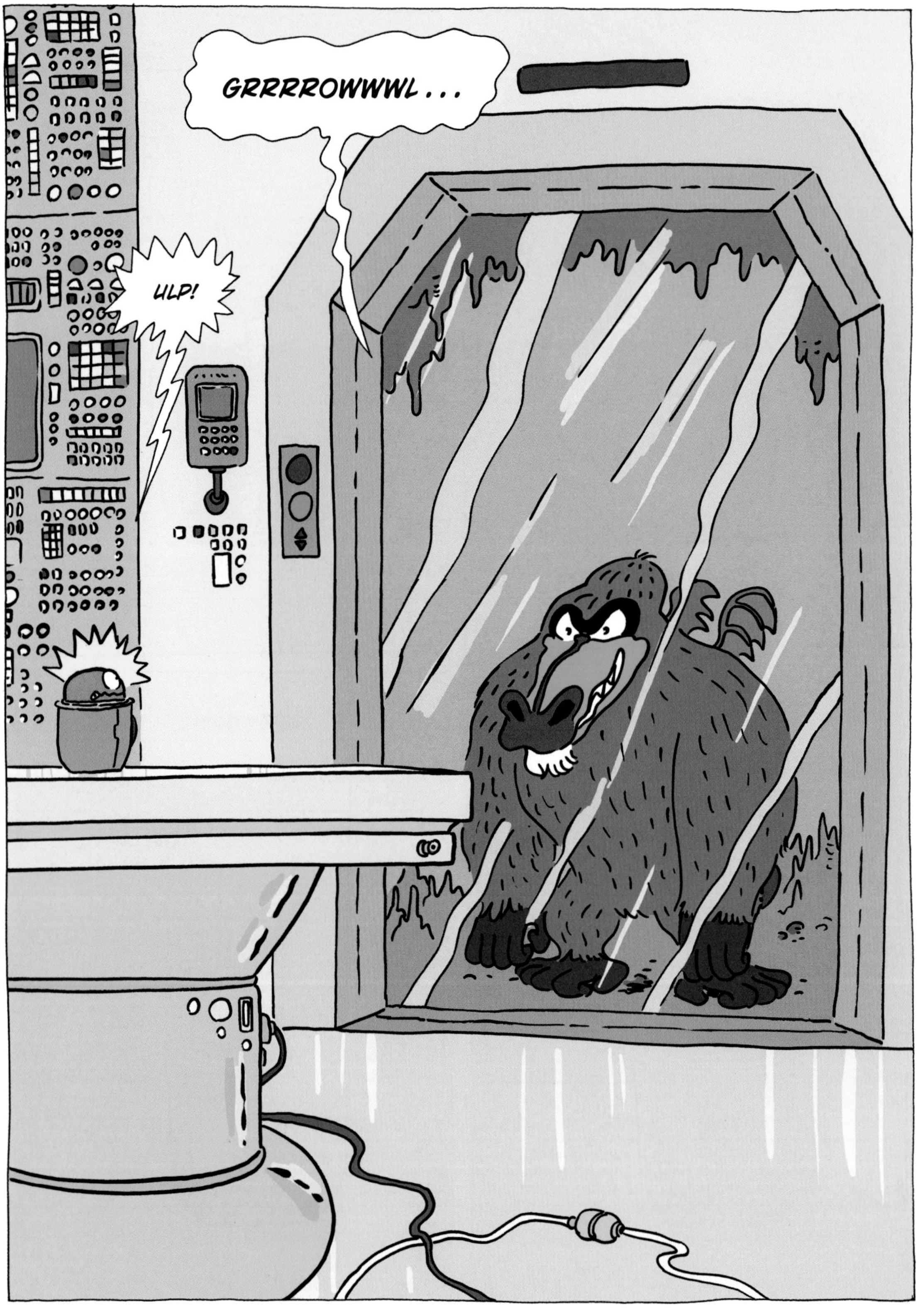
GRRRROWWWL . . .
ULP!

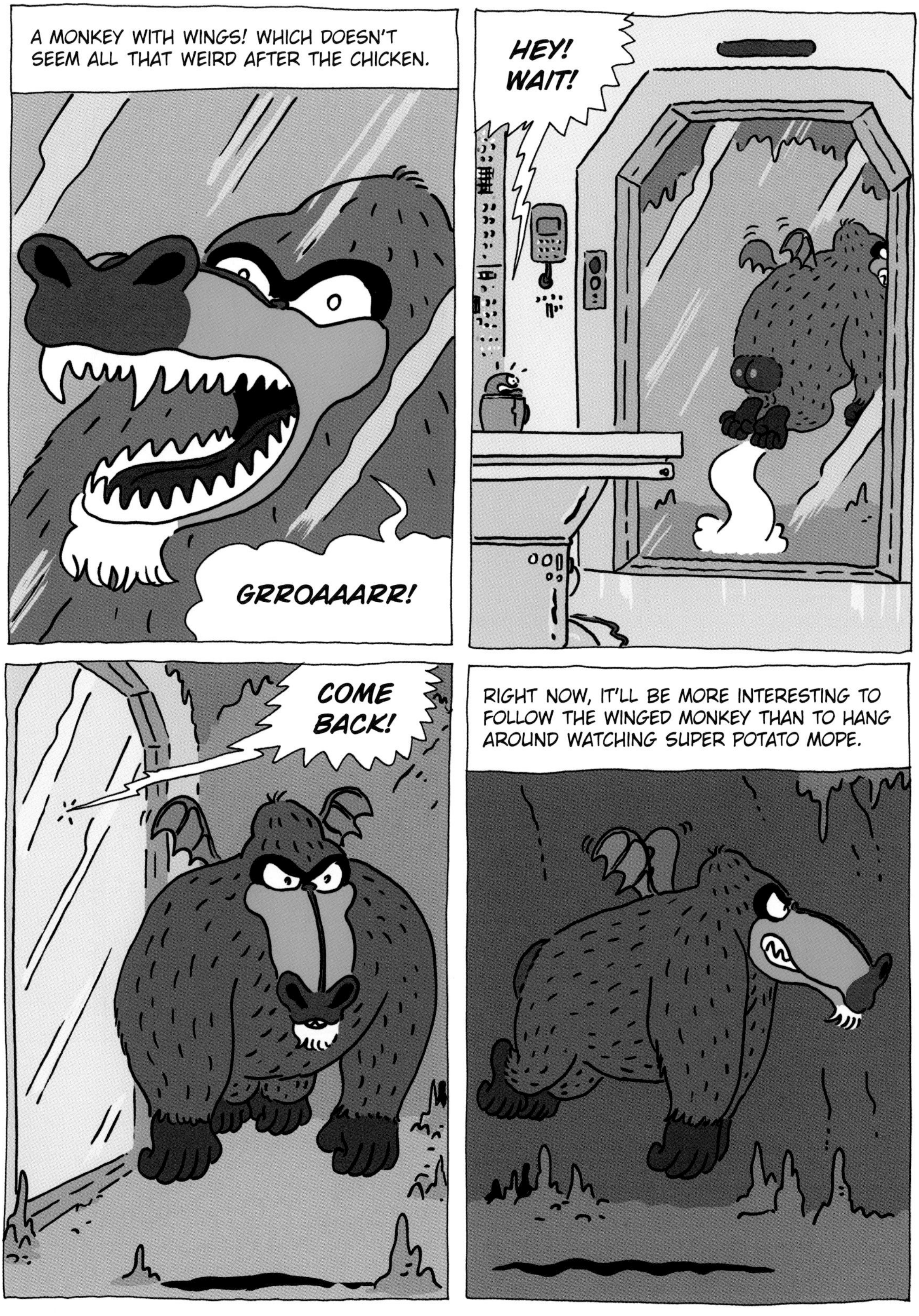

A MONKEY WITH WINGS! WHICH DOESN'T SEEM ALL THAT WEIRD AFTER THE CHICKEN.
GRROAAAARR!
HEY! WAIT!
COME BACK!
RIGHT NOW, IT'LL BE MORE INTERESTING TO FOLLOW THE WINGED MONKEY THAN TO HANG AROUND WATCHING SUPER POTATO MOPE.

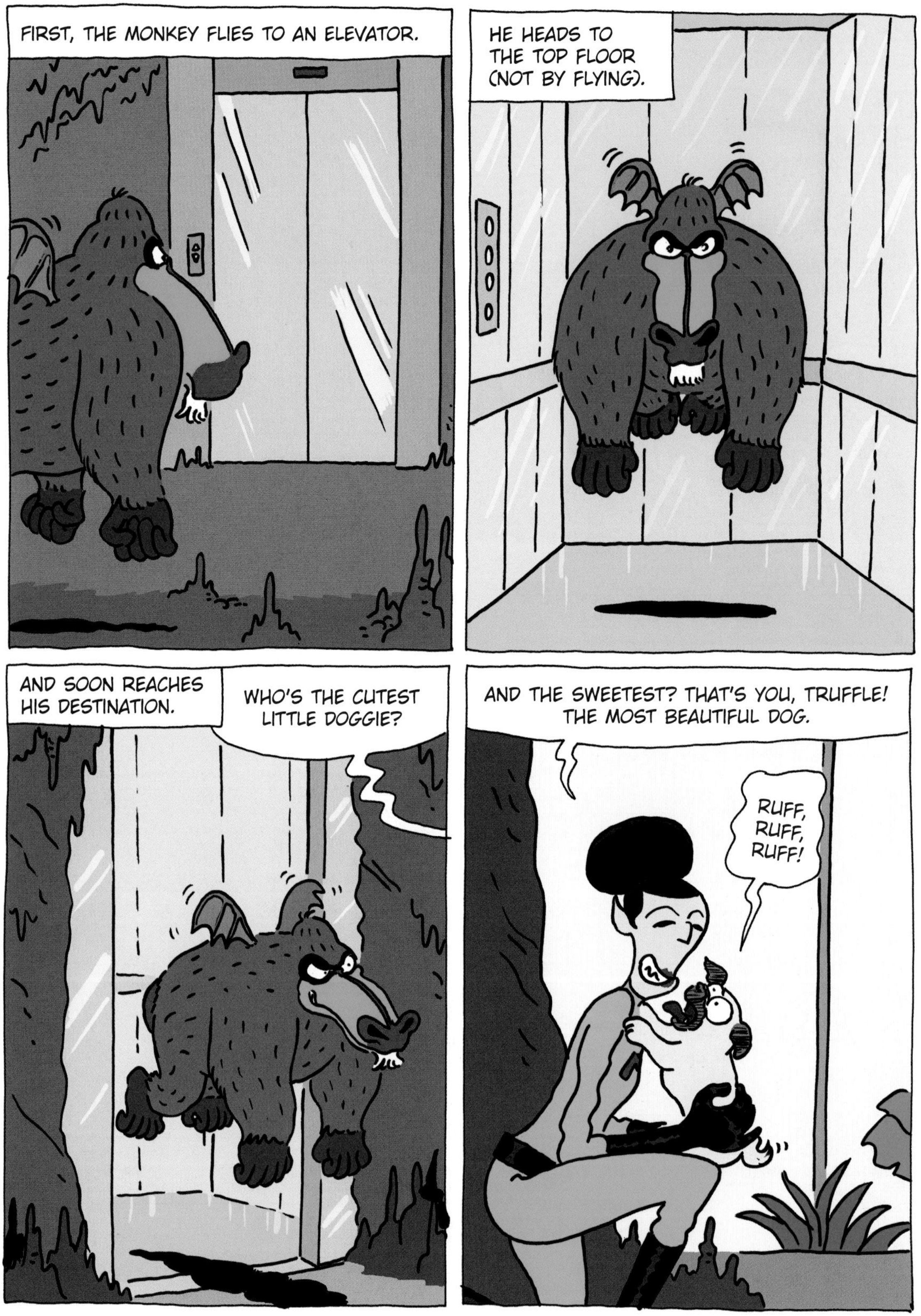
FIRST, THE MONKEY FLIES TO AN ELEVATOR.
HE HEADS TO THE TOP FLOOR (NOT BY FLYING).
AND SOON REACHES HIS DESTINATION.
WHO'S THE CUTEST LITTLE DOGGIE?
AND THE SWEETEST? THAT'S YOU, TRUFFLE! THE MOST BEAUTIFUL DOG.
RUFF, RUFF, RUFF!

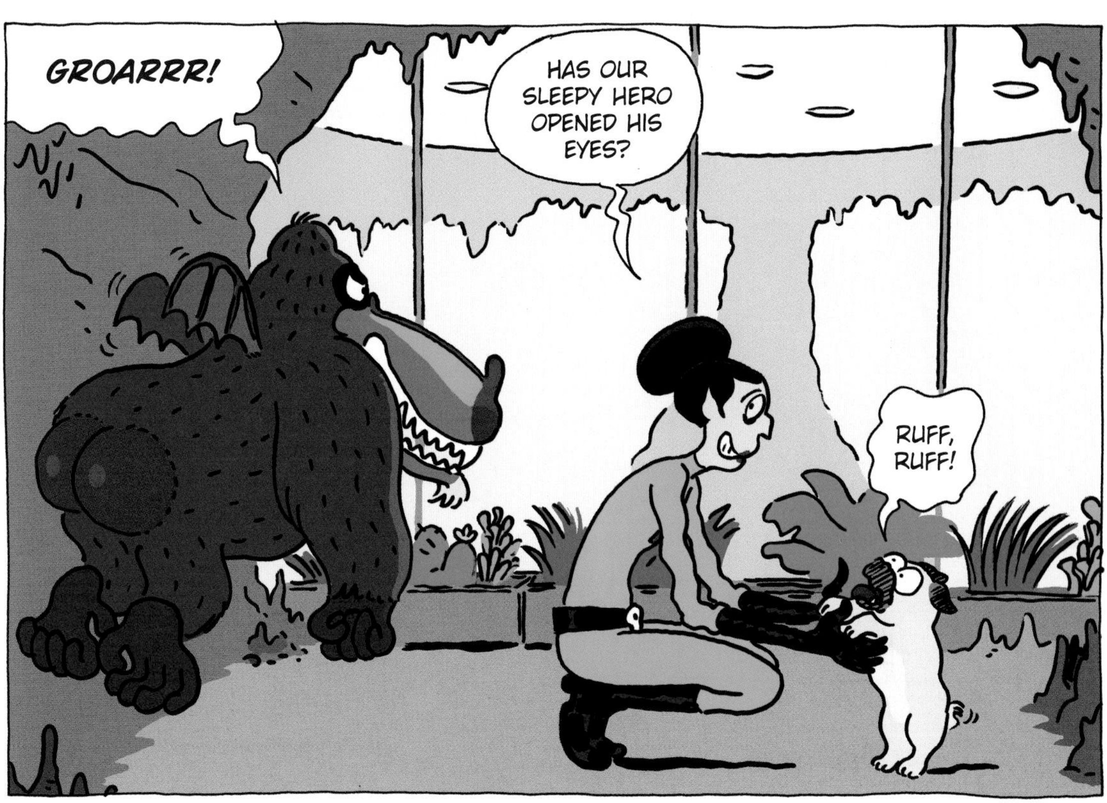
GROARRR!
HAS OUR SLEEPY HERO OPENED HIS EYES?
RUFF, RUFF!

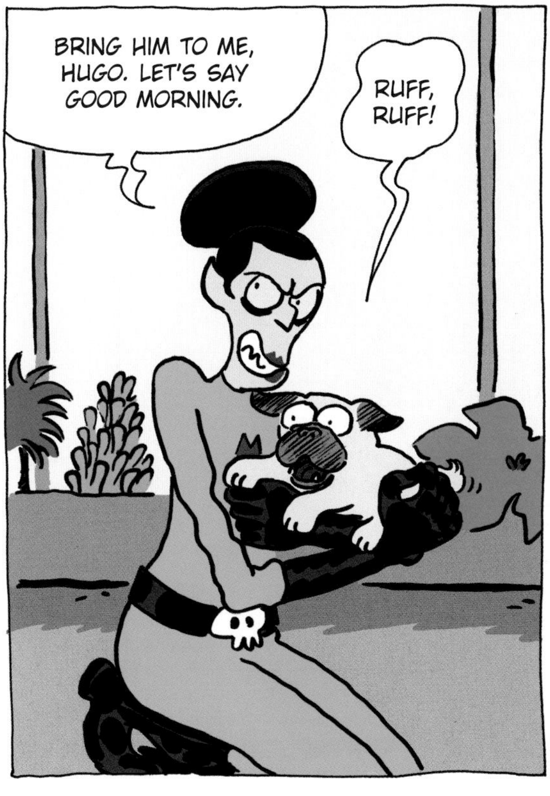
BRING HIM TO ME, HUGO. LET'S SAY GOOD MORNING.
RUFF, RUFF!

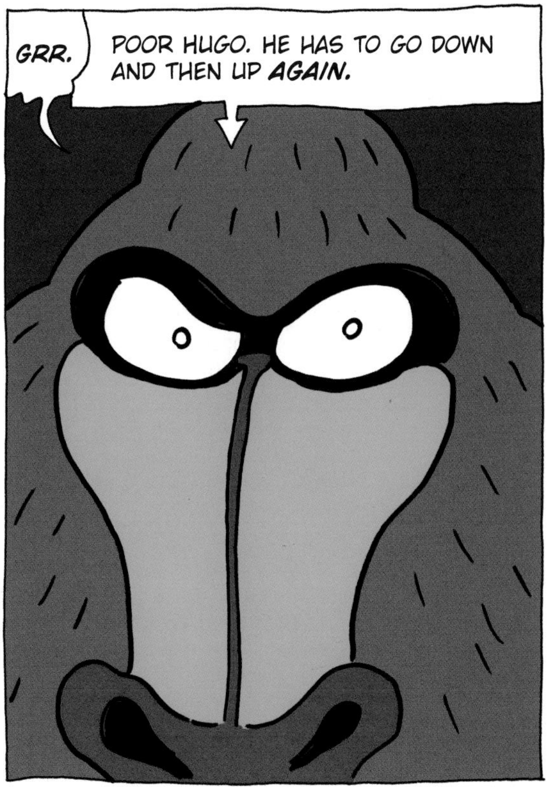
GRR.
POOR HUGO. HE HAS TO GO DOWN AND THEN UP AGAIN.

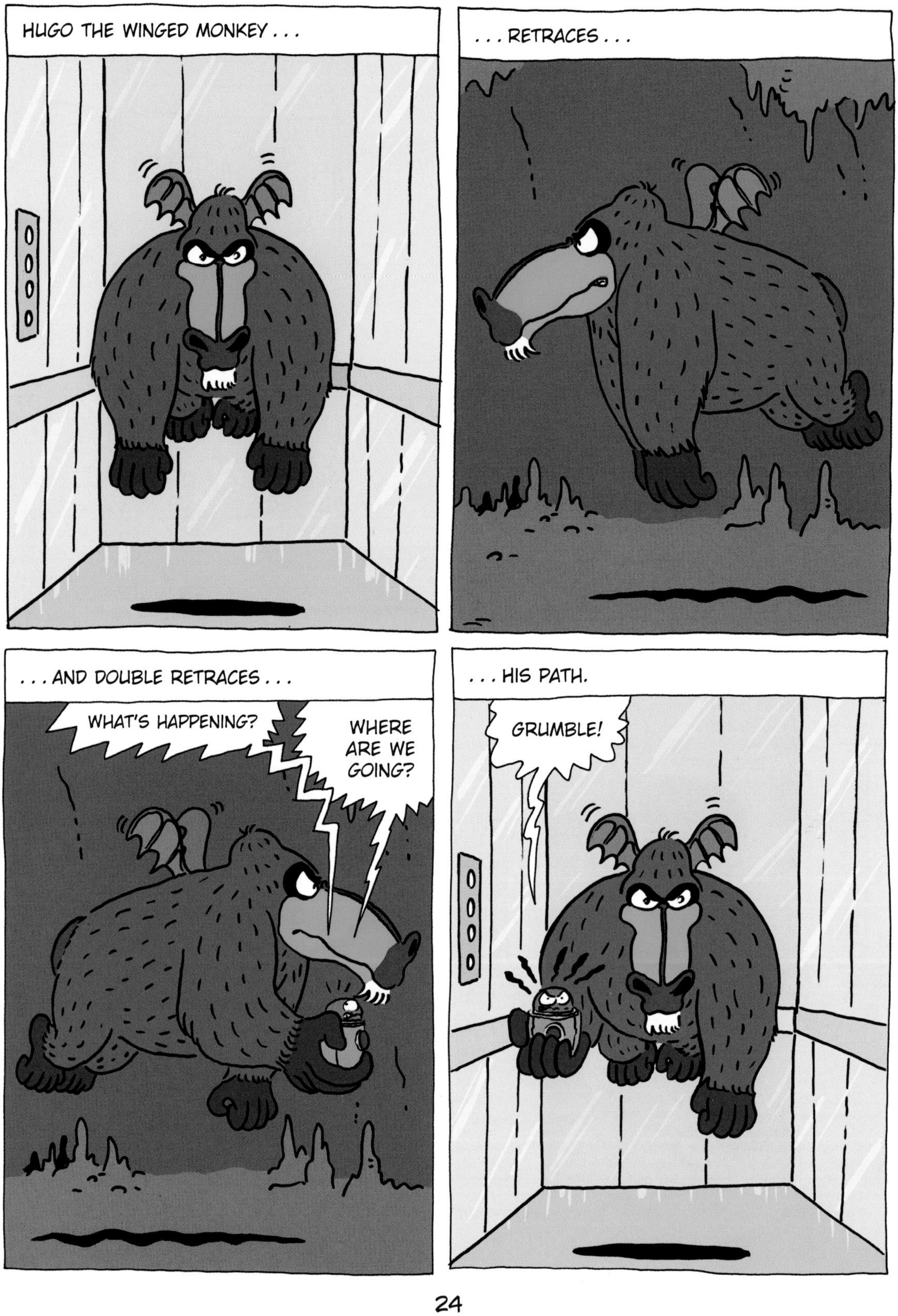
HUGO THE WINGED MONKEY . . .
. . . RETRACES . . .
. . . AND DOUBLE RETRACES . . .
WHAT'S HAPPENING?
WHERE ARE WE GOING?
. . . HIS PATH.
GRUMBLE!

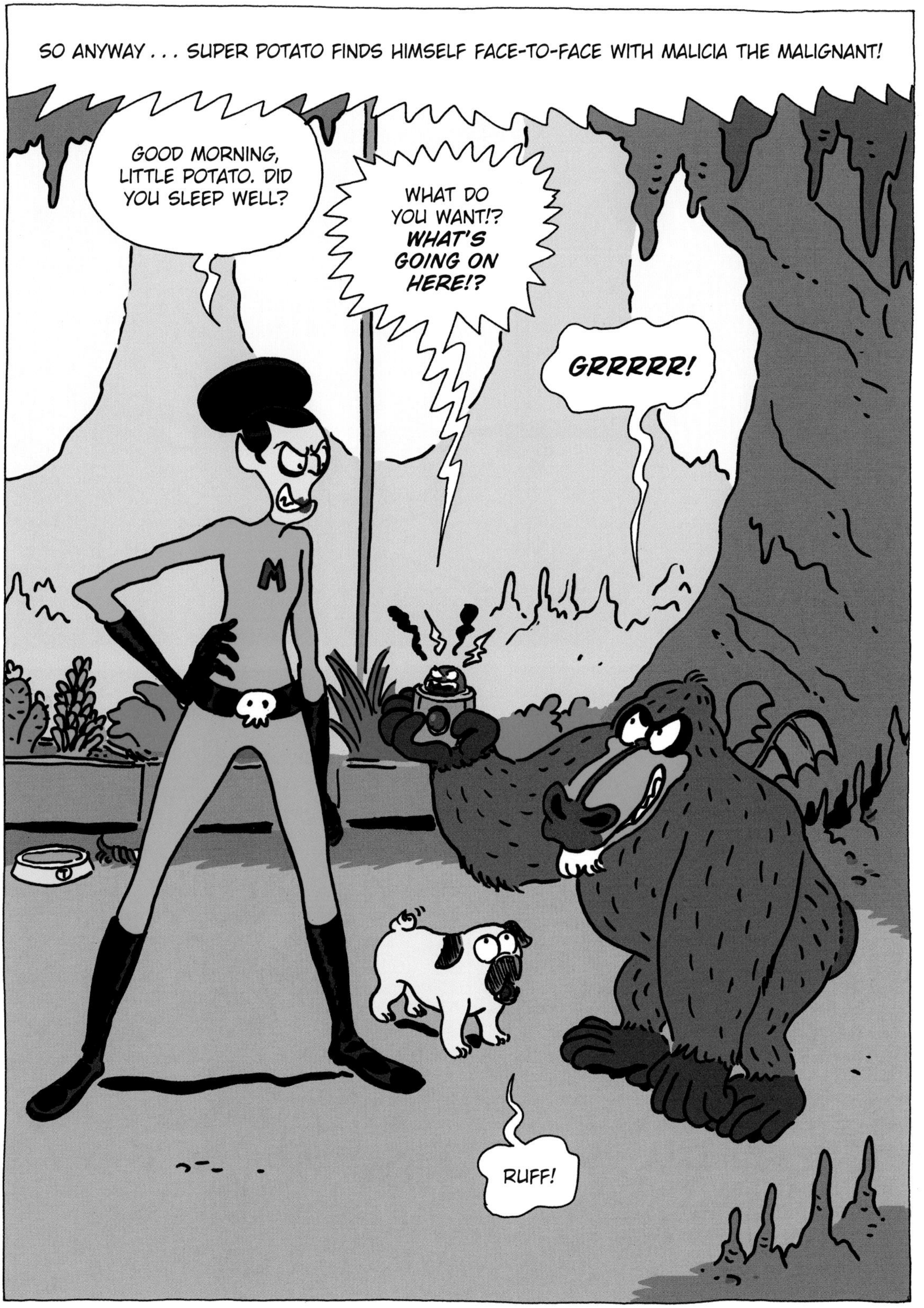
SO ANYWAY . . . SUPER POTATO FINDS HIMSELF FACE-TO-FACE WITH MALICIA THE MALIGNANT!
GOOD MORNING, LITTLE POTATO. DID YOU SLEEP WELL?
WHAT DO YOU WANT!? WHAT'S GOING ON HERE!?
GRRRRR!
RUFF!

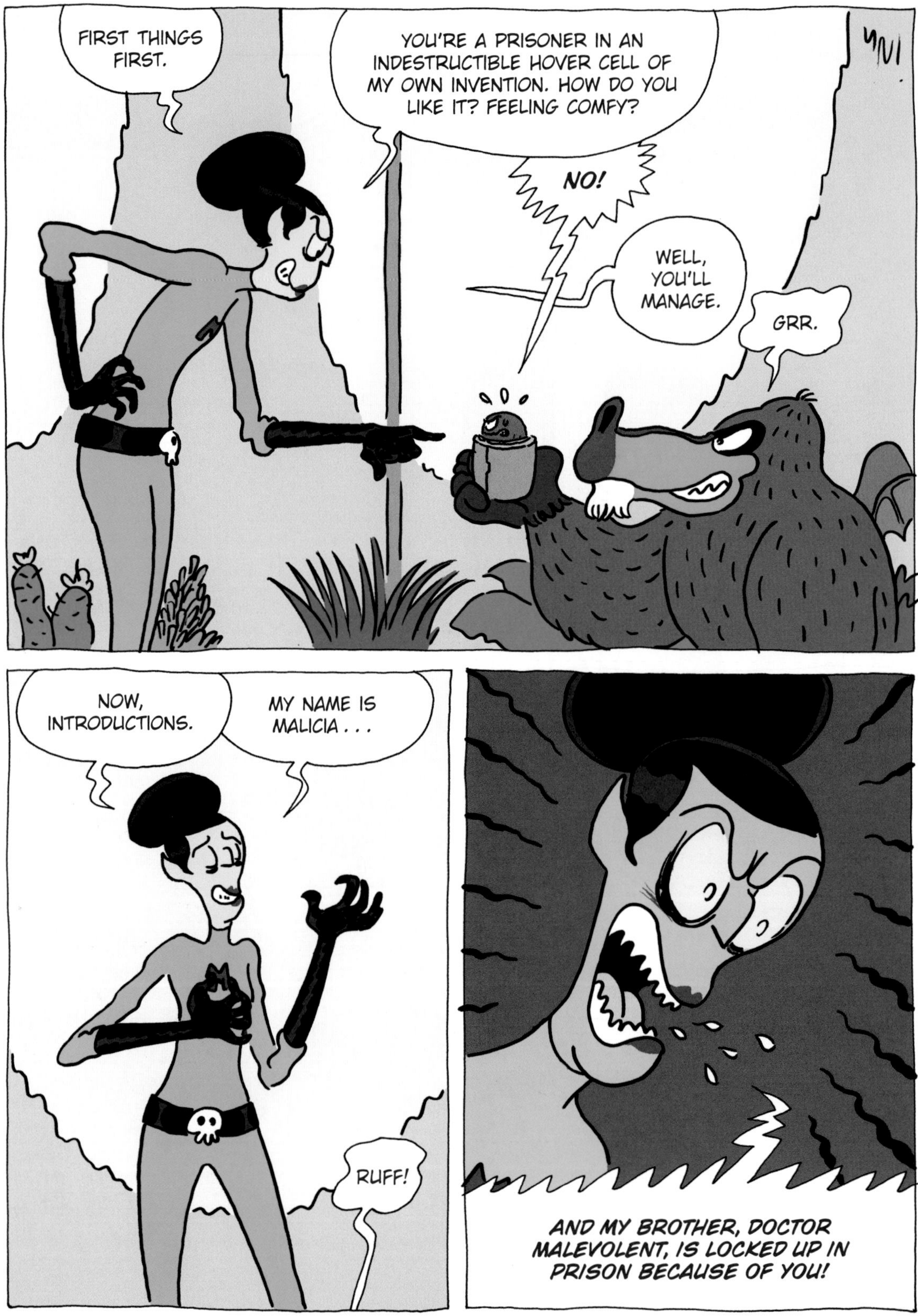
FIRST THINGS FIRST.
YOU'RE A PRISONER IN AN INDESTRUCTIBLE HOVER CELL OF MY OWN INVENTION. HOW DO YOU LIKE IT? FEELING COMFY?
NO!
WELL, YOU'LL MANAGE.
GRR.
NOW, INTRODUCTIONS.
MY NAME IS MALICIA . . .
RUFF!
AND MY BROTHER, DOCTOR MALEVOLENT, IS LOCKED UP IN PRISON BECAUSE OF YOU!

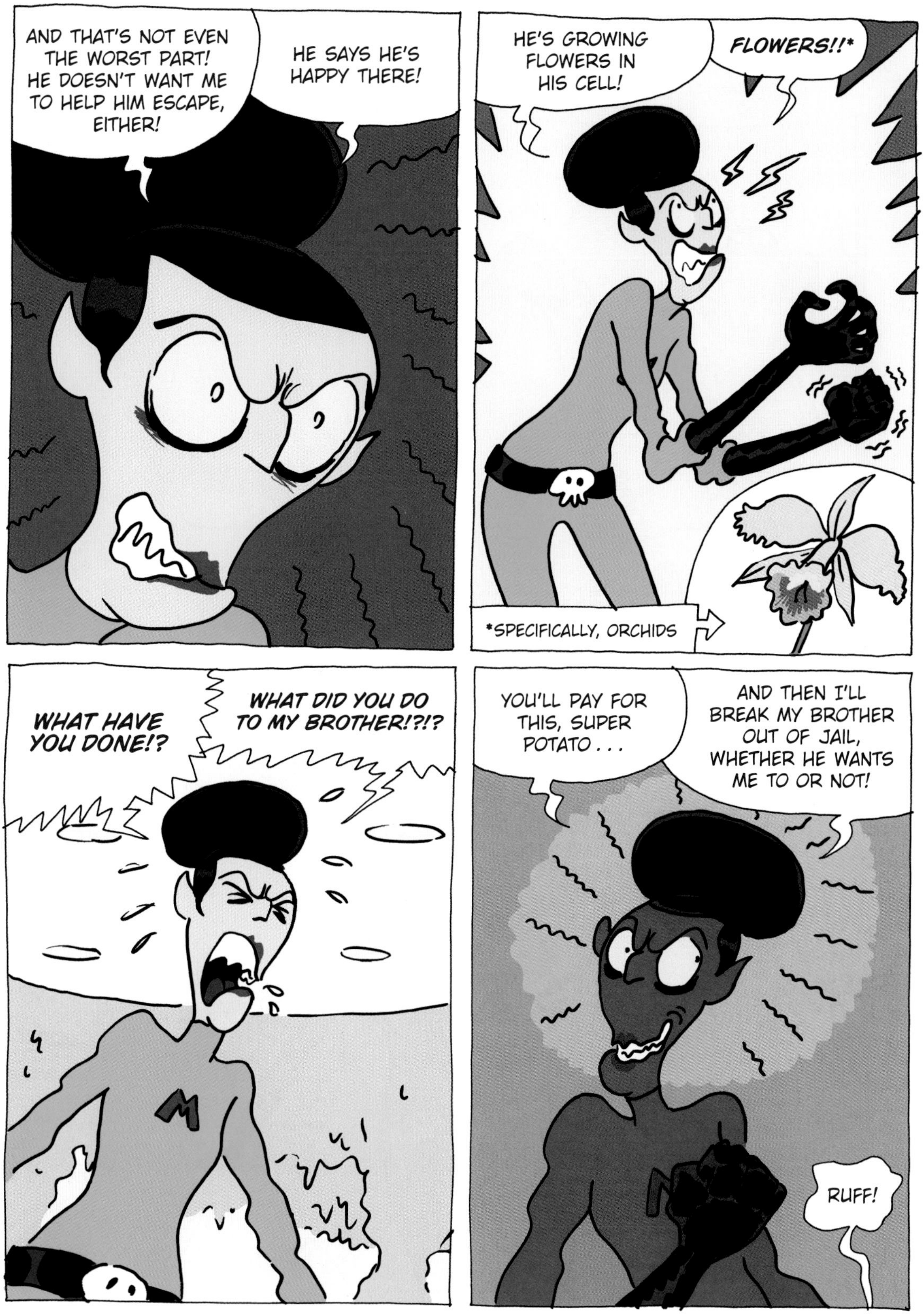
AND THAT'S NOT EVEN THE WORST PART! HE DOESN'T WANT ME TO HELP HIM ESCAPE, EITHER!
HE SAYS HE'S HAPPY THERE!
HE'S GROWING FLOWERS IN HIS CELL!
FLOWERS!!*
*SPECIFICALLY, ORCHIDS
WHAT HAVE YOU DONE!?
WHAT DID YOU DO TO MY BROTHER!?!?
YOU'LL PAY FOR THIS, SUPER POTATO . . .
AND THEN I'LL BREAK MY BROTHER OUT OF JAIL, WHETHER HE WANTS ME TO OR NOT!
RUFF!

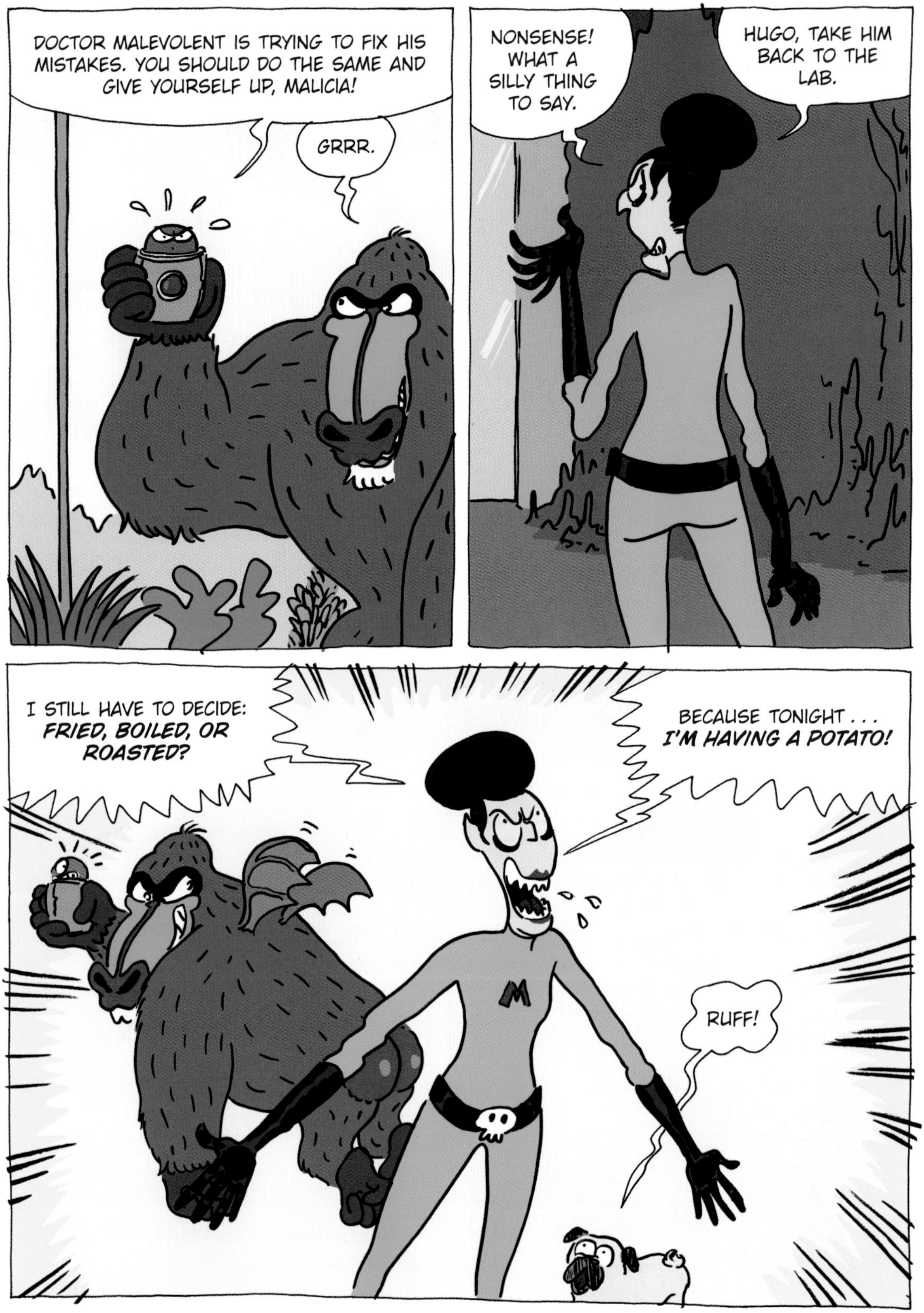
DOCTOR MALEVOLENT IS TRYING TO FIX HIS MISTAKES. YOU SHOULD DO THE SAME AND GIVE YOURSELF UP, MALICIA!
GRRR.
NONSENSE! WHAT A SILLY THING TO SAY.
HUGO, TAKE HIM BACK TO THE LAB.
I STILL HAVE TO DECIDE: *FRIED, BOILED, OR ROASTED?*
BECAUSE TONIGHT . . . *I'M HAVING A POTATO!*
RUFF!

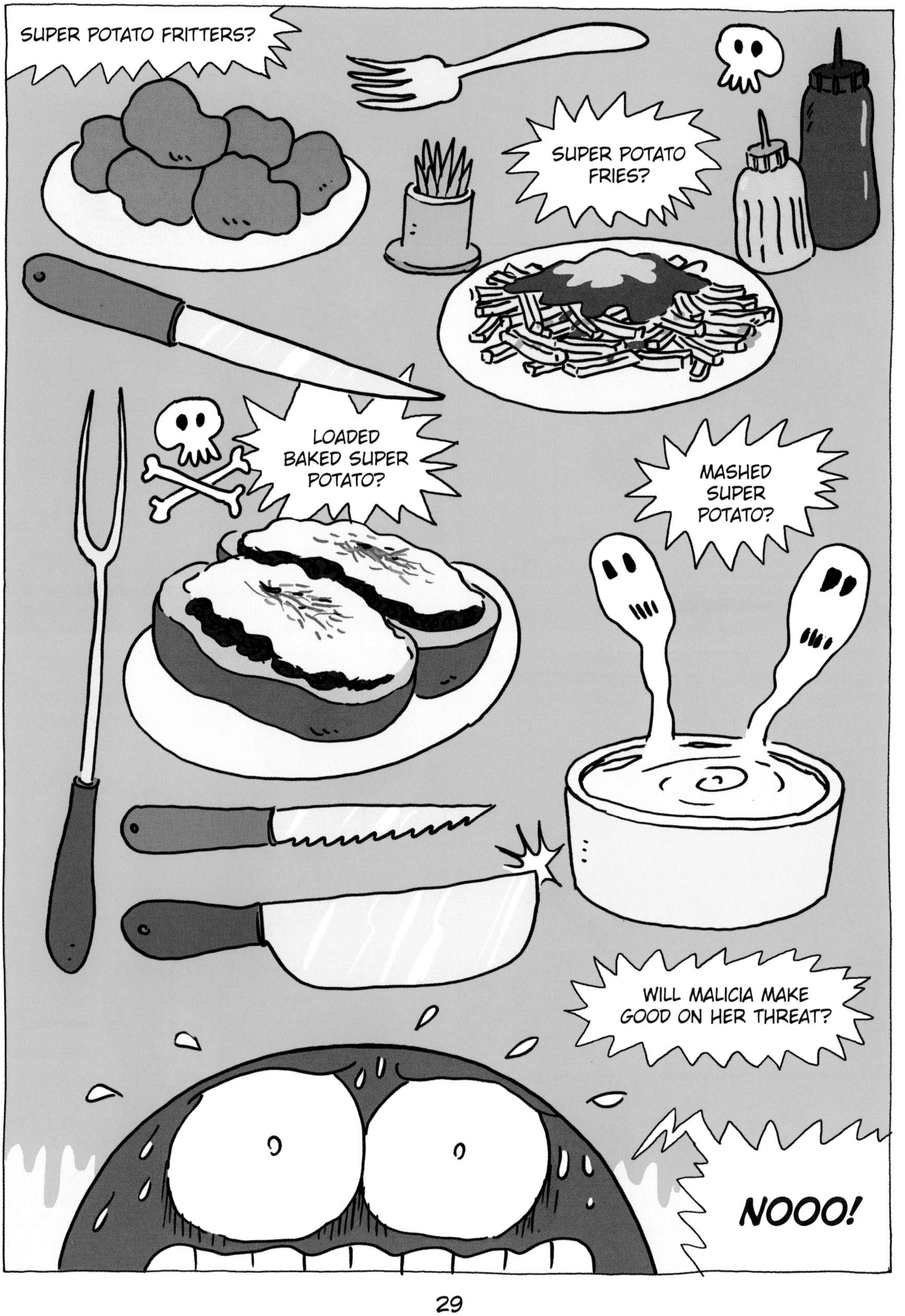
SUPER POTATO FRITTERS?
SUPER POTATO FRIES?
LOADED BAKED SUPER POTATO?
MASHED SUPER POTATO?
WILL MALICIA MAKE GOOD ON HER THREAT?
NOOO!

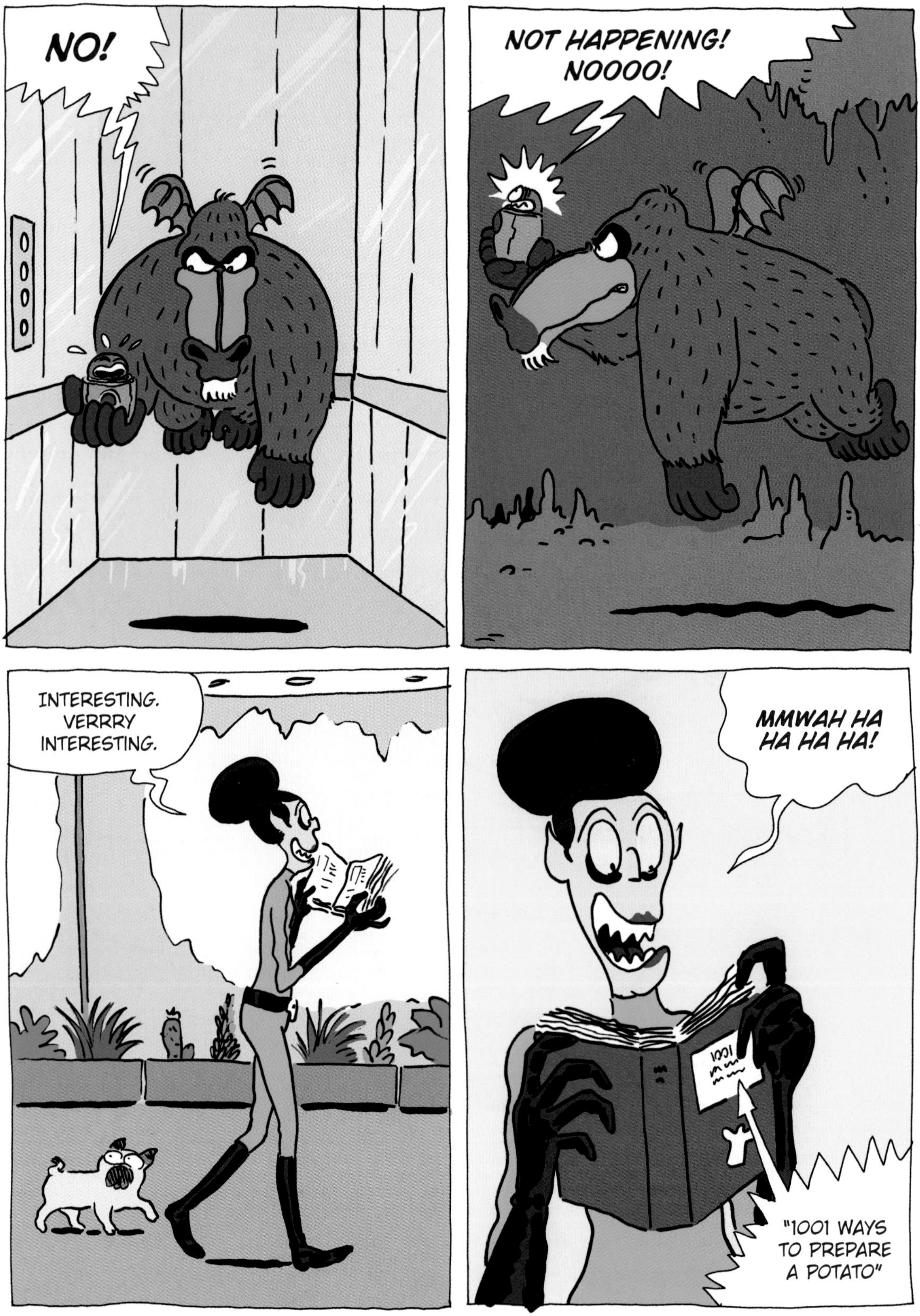
NO!
NOT HAPPENING! NOOOO!
INTERESTING. VERRRY INTERESTING.
MMWAH HA HA HA HA!
"1001 WAYS TO PREPARE A POTATO"

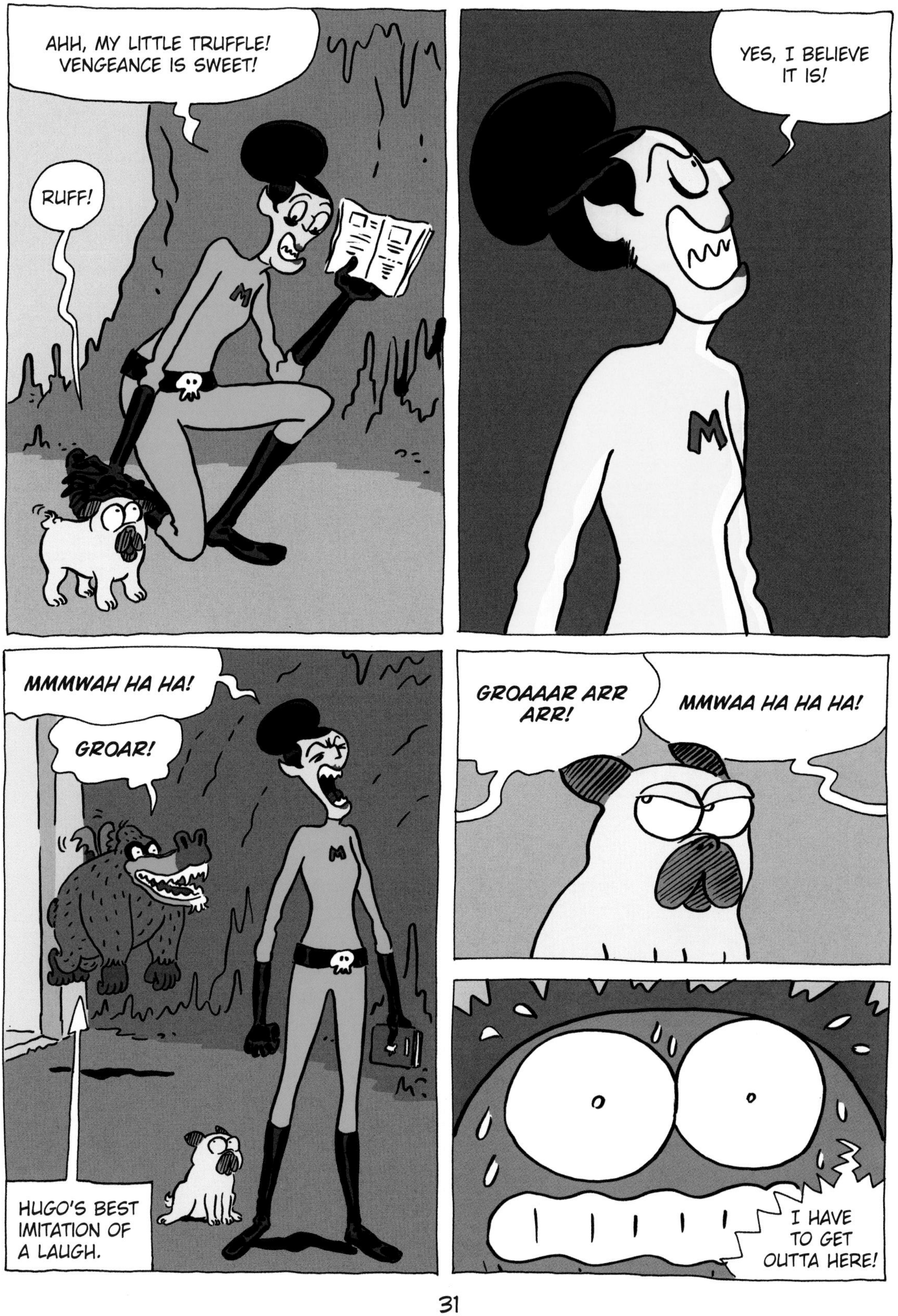
AHH, MY LITTLE TRUFFLE! VENGEANCE IS SWEET!
RUFF!
YES, I BELIEVE IT IS!
MMMWAH HA HA!
GROAR!
HUGO'S BEST IMITATION OF A LAUGH.
GROAAAR ARR ARR!
MMWAA HA HA HA!
I HAVE TO GET OUTTA HERE!

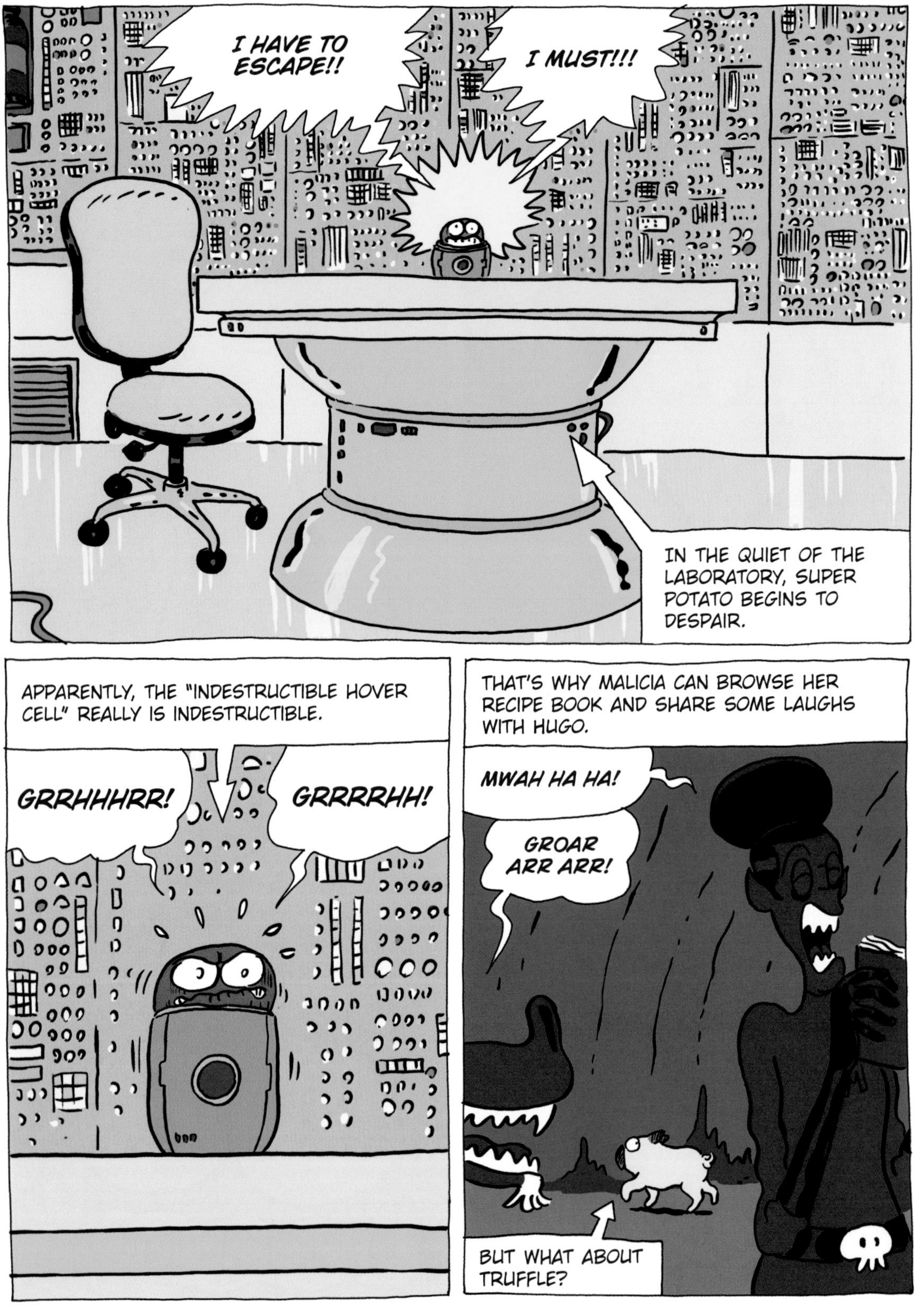
I HAVE TO ESCAPE!!
I MUST!!!
IN THE QUIET OF THE LABORATORY, SUPER POTATO BEGINS TO DESPAIR.
APPARENTLY, THE "INDESTRUCTIBLE HOVER CELL" REALLY IS INDESTRUCTIBLE.
GRRHHHRR!
GRRRRHH!
THAT'S WHY MALICIA CAN BROWSE HER RECIPE BOOK AND SHARE SOME LAUGHS WITH HUGO.
MWAH HA HA!
GROAR ARR ARR!
BUT WHAT ABOUT TRUFFLE?

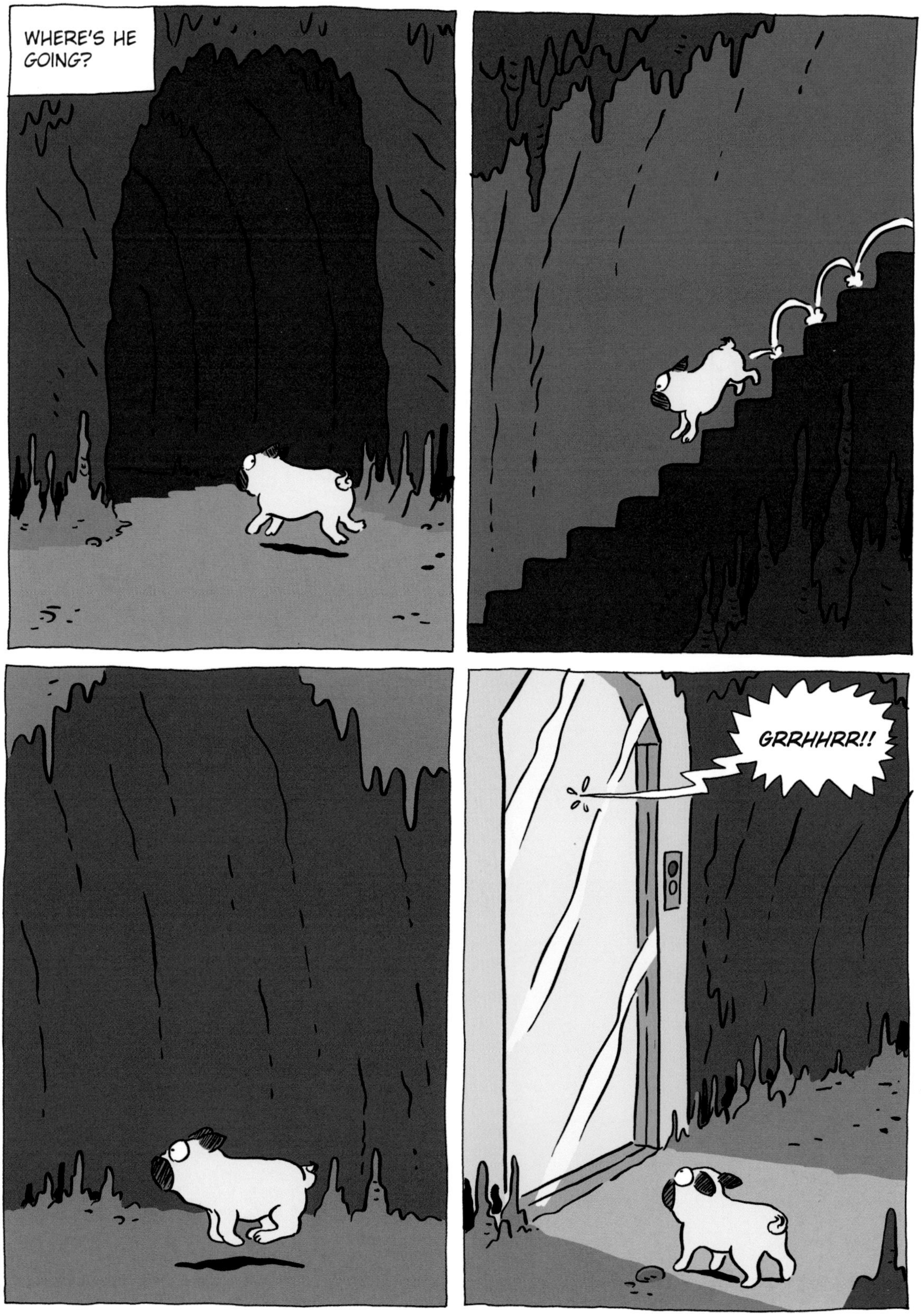
WHERE'S HE GOING?
GRRHHRR!!

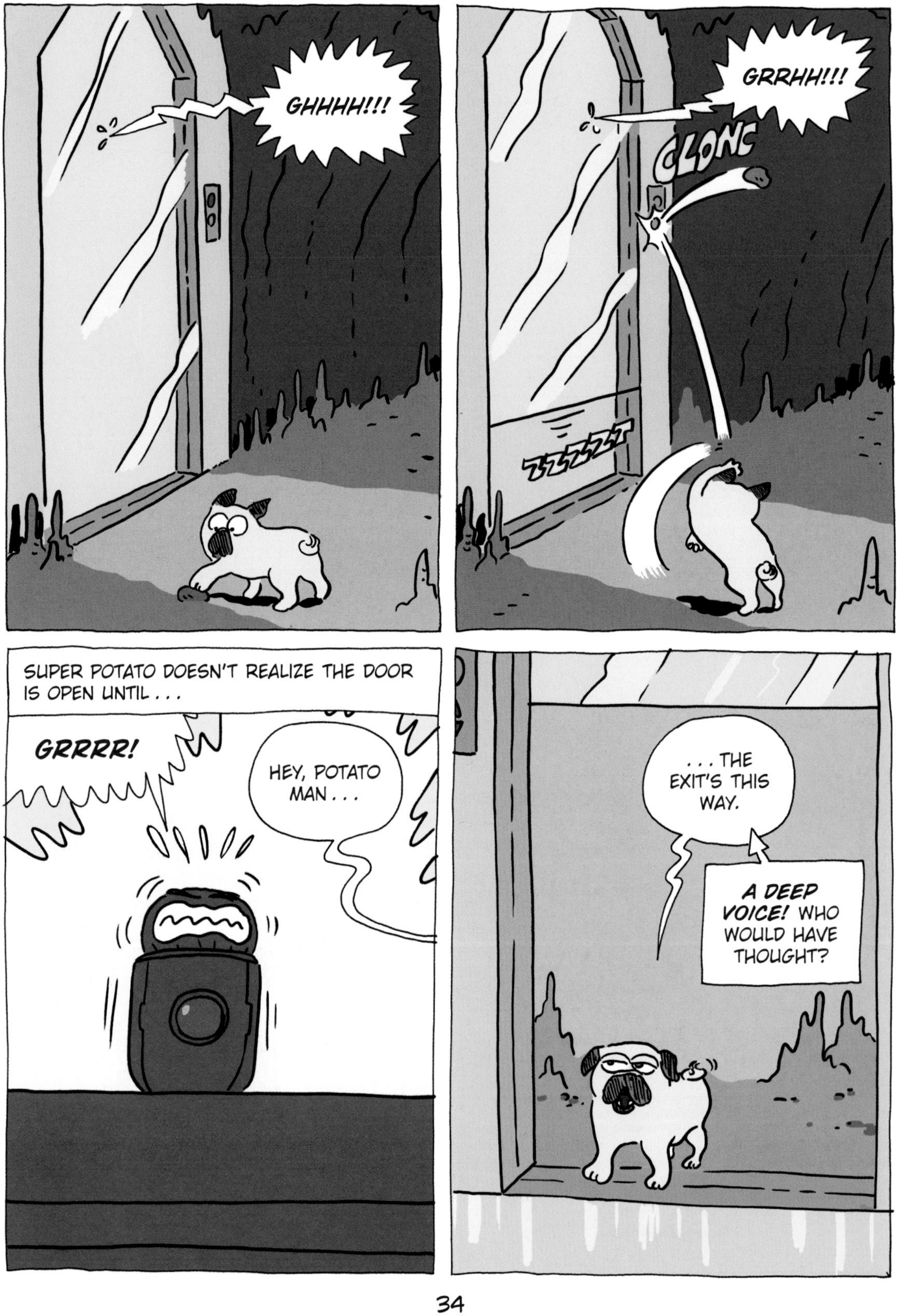
GHHHH!!!
GRRHH!!!
CLONC
ZZZZZZ
SUPER POTATO DOESN'T REALIZE THE DOOR IS OPEN UNTIL . . .
GRRRR!
HEY, POTATO MAN . . .
. . . THE EXIT'S THIS WAY.
A DEEP VOICE! WHO WOULD HAVE THOUGHT?

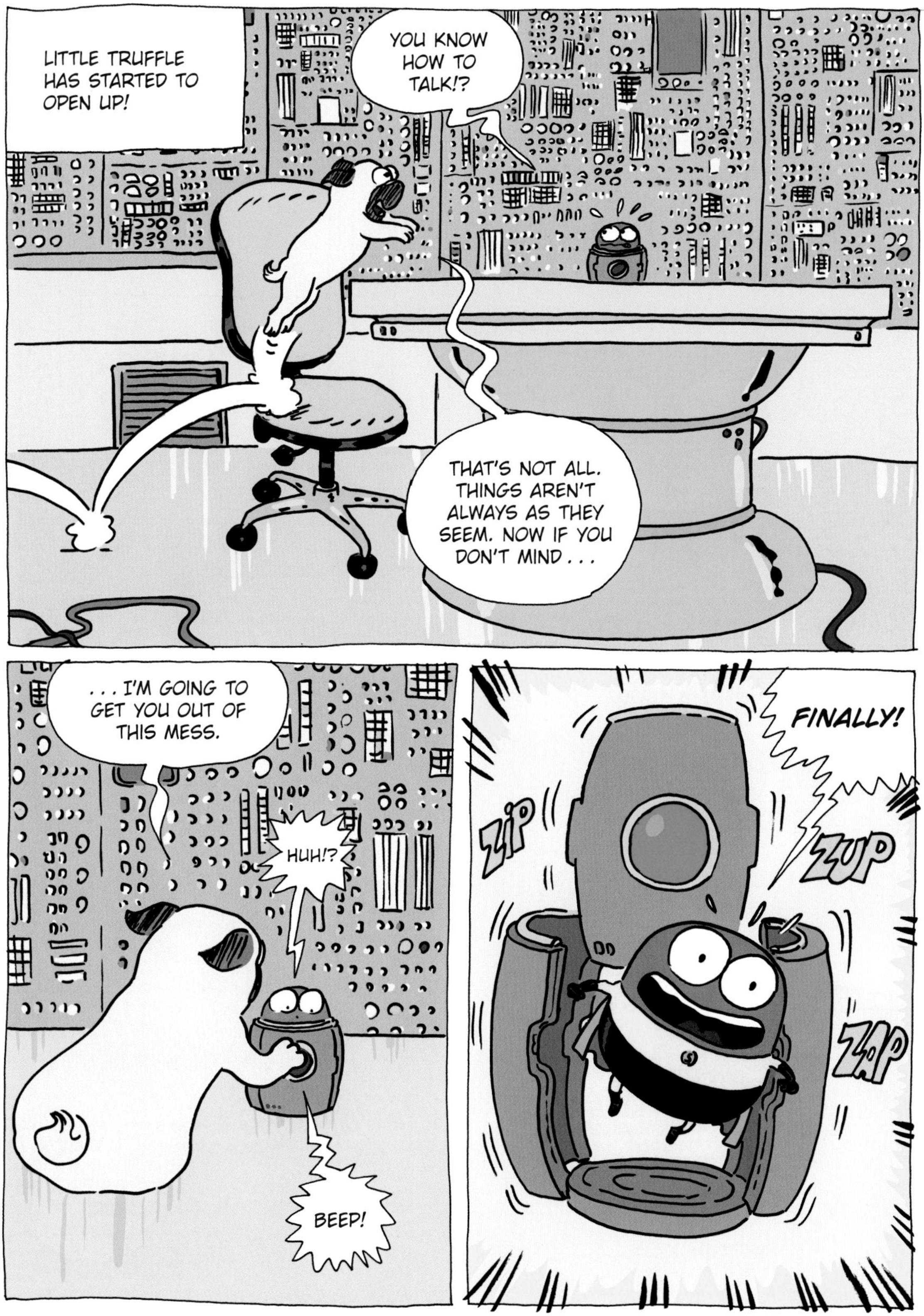
LITTLE TRUFFLE HAS STARTED TO OPEN UP!
YOU KNOW HOW TO TALK!?
THAT'S NOT ALL. THINGS AREN'T ALWAYS AS THEY SEEM. NOW IF YOU DON'T MIND . . .
. . . I'M GOING TO GET YOU OUT OF THIS MESS.
HUH!?
BEEP!
FINALLY!
ZIP
ZUP
ZAP

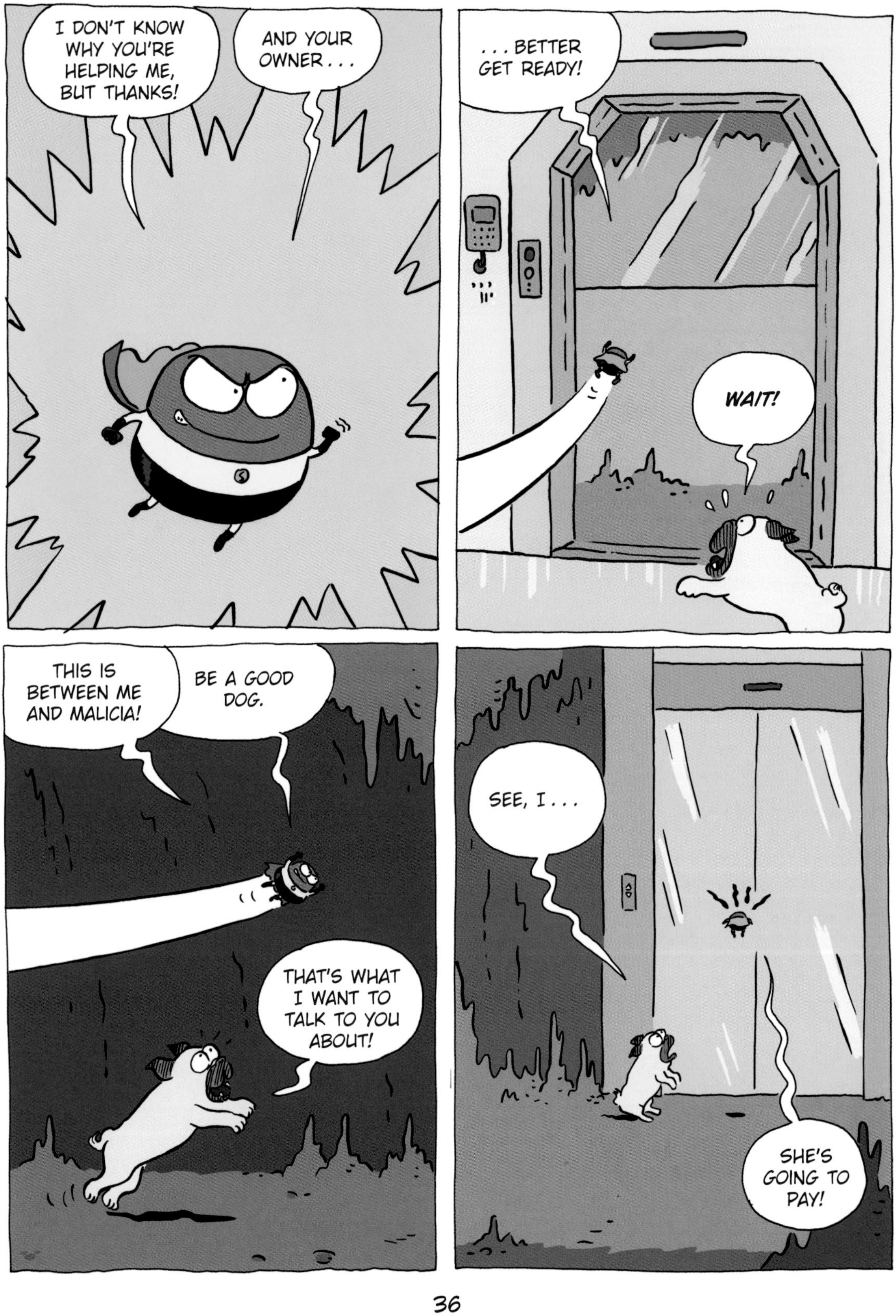
I DON'T KNOW WHY YOU'RE HELPING ME, BUT THANKS!
AND YOUR OWNER . . .
. . . BETTER GET READY!
WAIT!
THIS IS BETWEEN ME AND MALICIA!
BE A GOOD DOG.
THAT'S WHAT I WANT TO TALK TO YOU ABOUT!
SEE, I . . .
SHE'S GOING TO PAY!

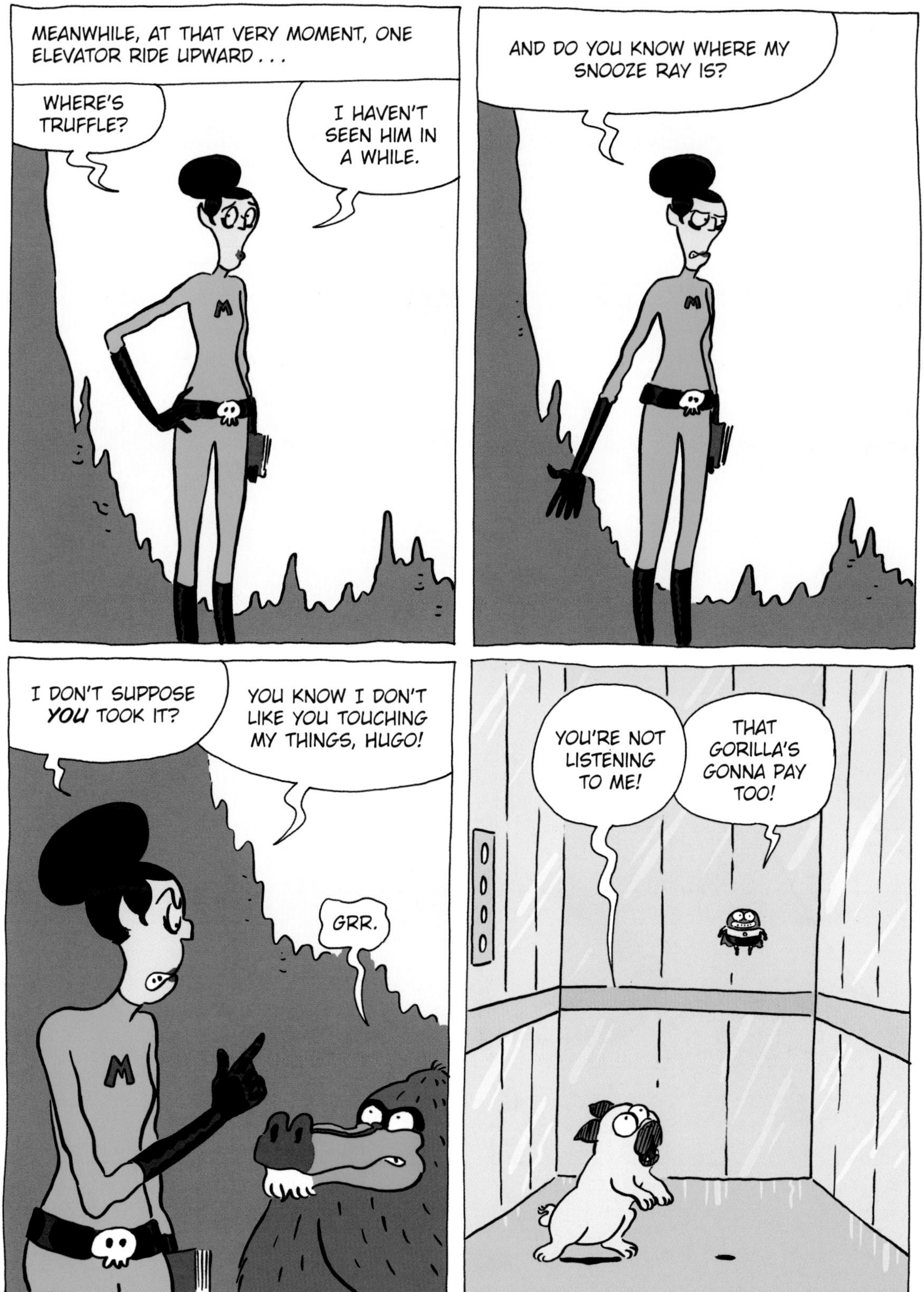
MEANWHILE, AT THAT VERY MOMENT, ONE ELEVATOR RIDE UPWARD . . .
WHERE'S TRUFFLE?
I HAVEN'T SEEN HIM IN A WHILE.
AND DO YOU KNOW WHERE MY SNOOZE RAY IS?
I DON'T SUPPOSE *YOU* TOOK IT?
YOU KNOW I DON'T LIKE YOU TOUCHING MY THINGS, HUGO!
GRR.
YOU'RE NOT LISTENING TO ME!
THAT GORILLA'S GONNA PAY TOO!

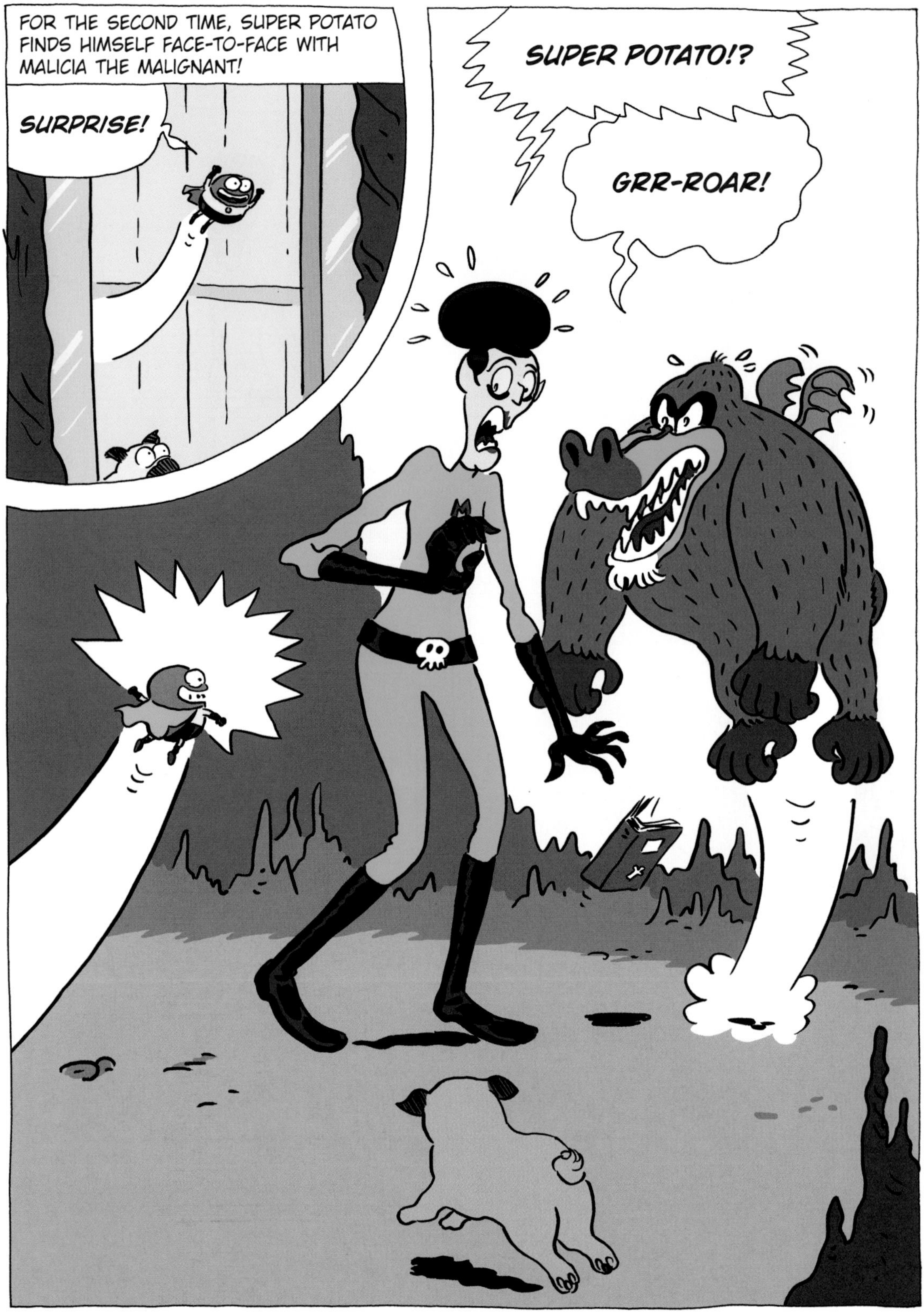
FOR THE SECOND TIME, SUPER POTATO FINDS HIMSELF FACE-TO-FACE WITH MALICIA THE MALIGNANT!
SURPRISE!
SUPER POTATO!?
GRR-ROAR!

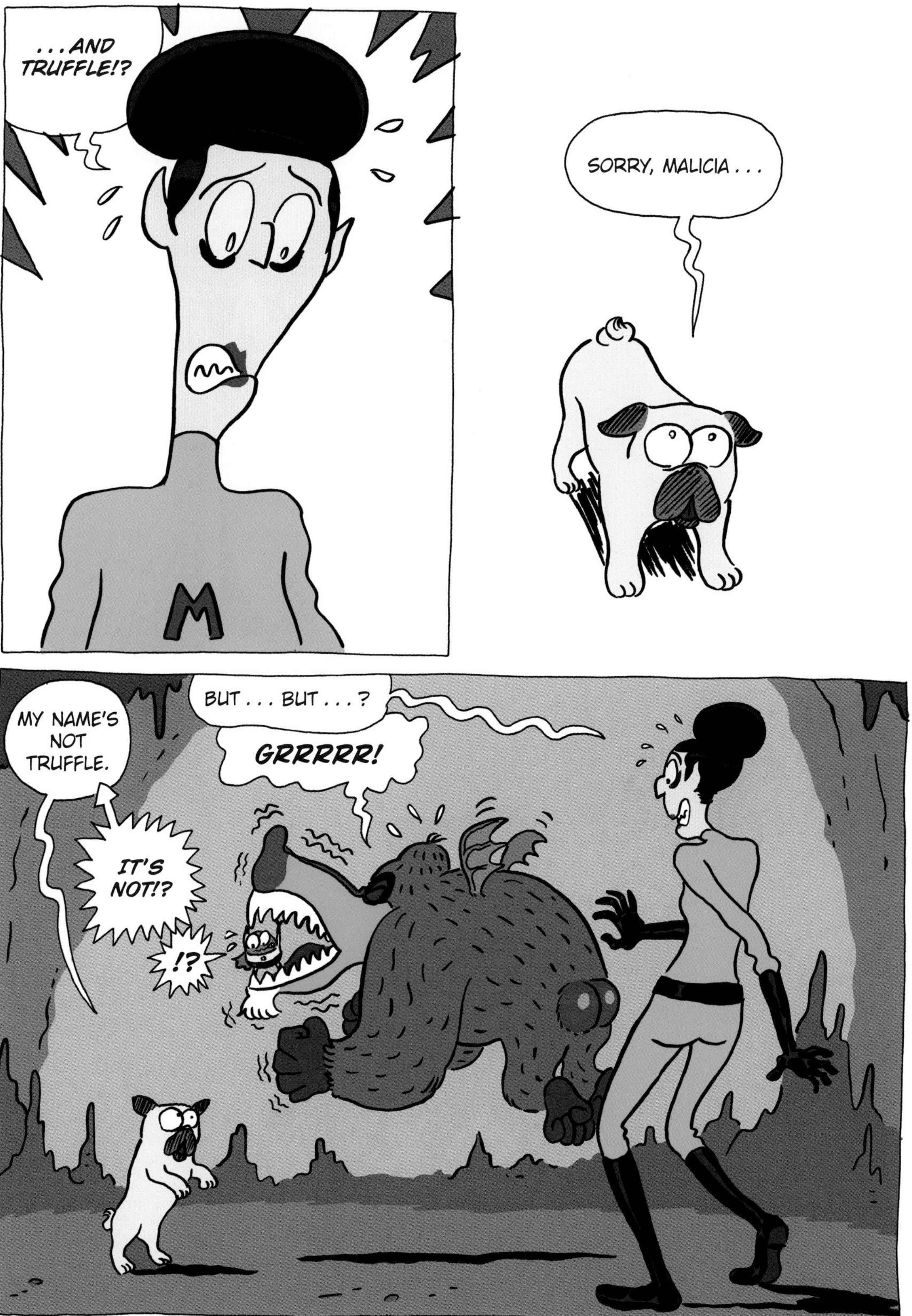
. . . AND TRUFFLE!?
SORRY, MALICIA . . .
MY NAME'S NOT TRUFFLE.
IT'S NOT!?
!?
BUT . . . BUT . . . ?
GRRRRR!

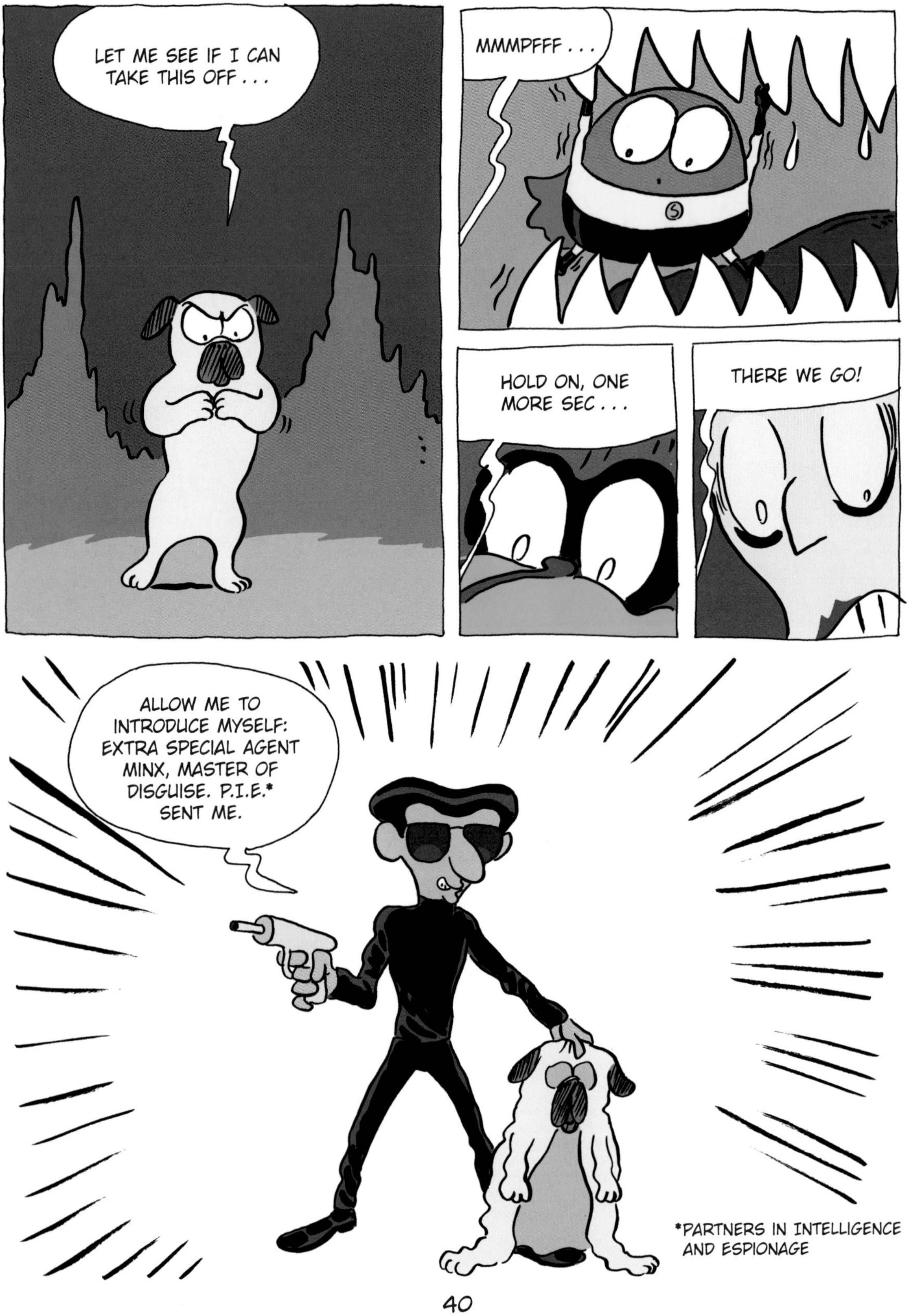
LET ME SEE IF I CAN TAKE THIS OFF . . .
MMMPFFF . . .
HOLD ON, ONE MORE SEC . . .
THERE WE GO!
ALLOW ME TO INTRODUCE MYSELF: EXTRA SPECIAL AGENT MINX, MASTER OF DISGUISE. P.I.E.* SENT ME.
*PARTNERS IN INTELLIGENCE AND ESPIONAGE

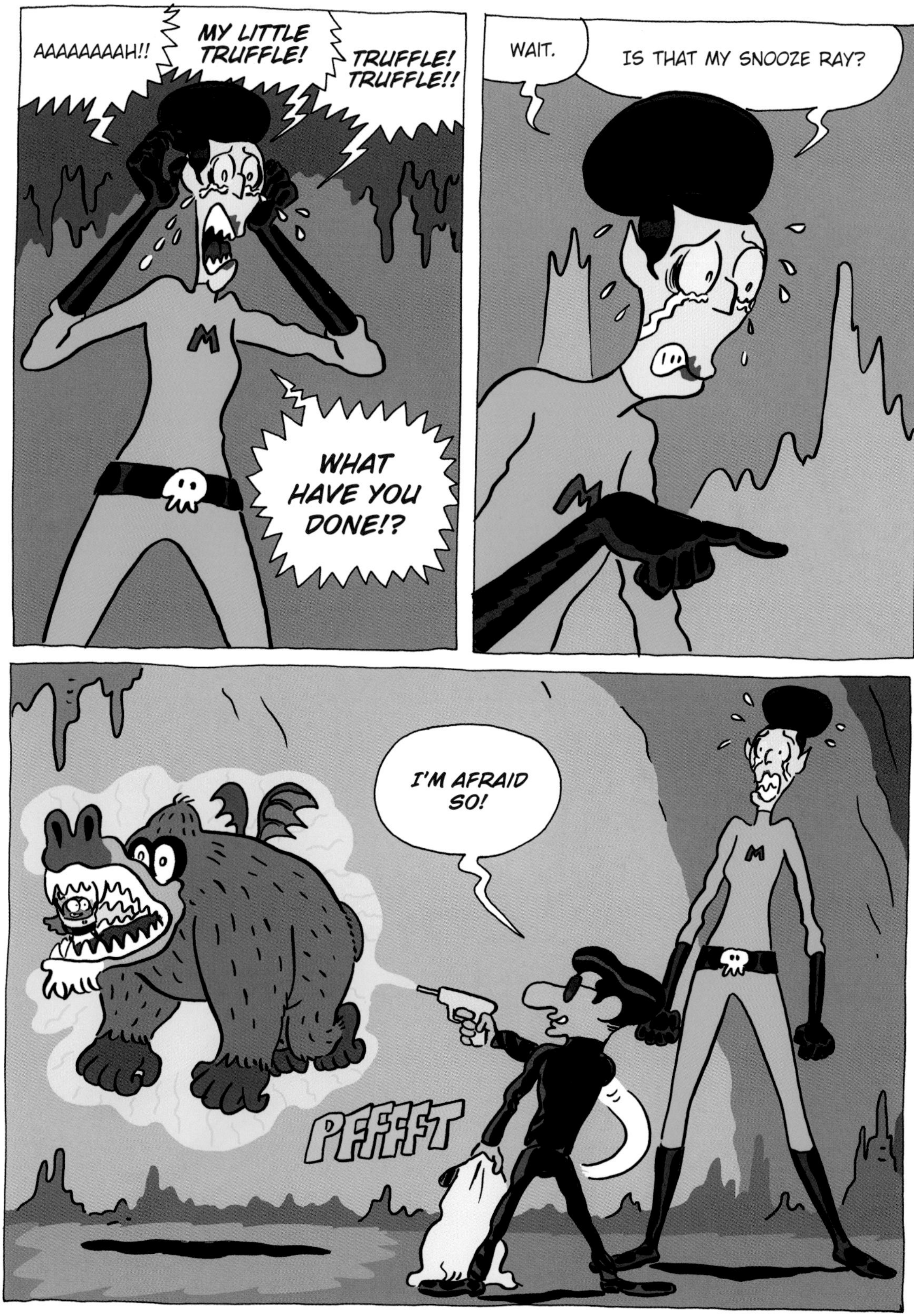
AAAAAAAAAH!!
MY LITTLE TRUFFLE!
TRUFFLE! TRUFFLE!!
WHAT HAVE YOU DONE!?
WAIT.
IS THAT MY SNOOZE RAY?
I'M AFRAID SO!
PFFFFT

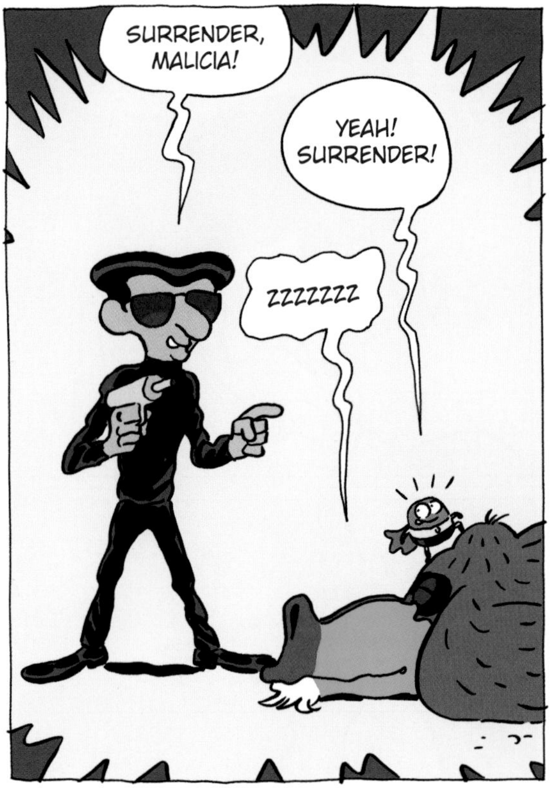
SURRENDER, MALICIA!
YEAH! SURRENDER!
ZZZZZZZ

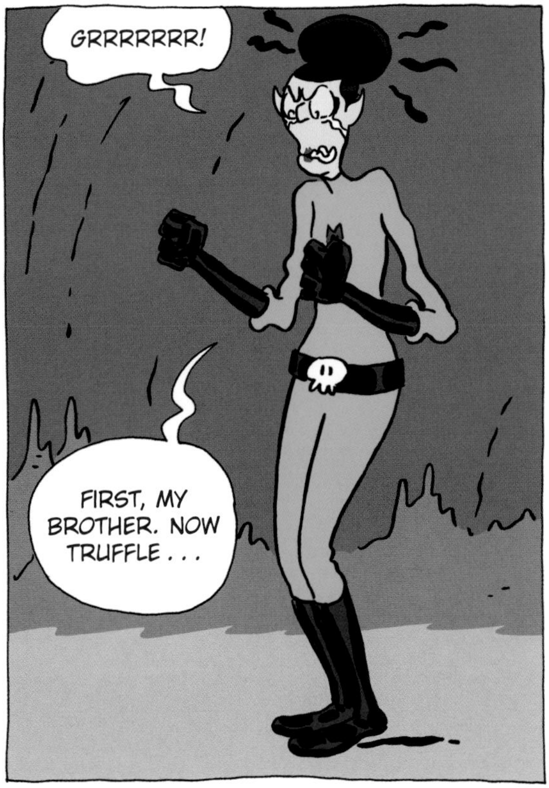
GRRRRRRR!
FIRST, MY BROTHER. NOW TRUFFLE . . .

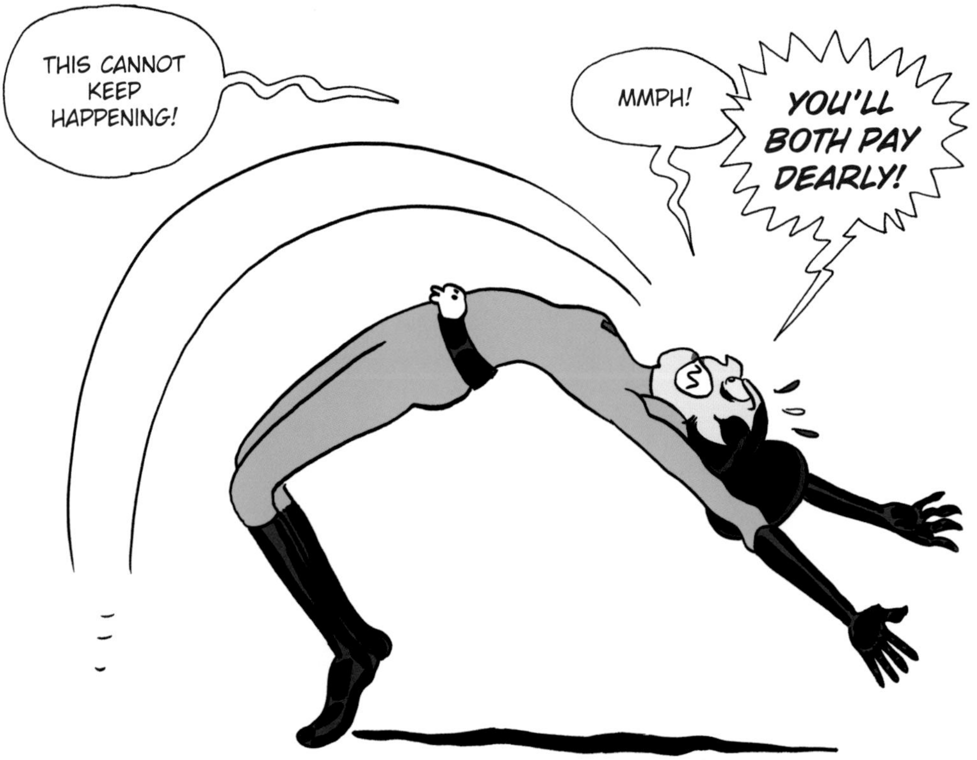
THIS CANNOT KEEP HAPPENING!
MMPH!
YOU'LL BOTH PAY DEARLY!

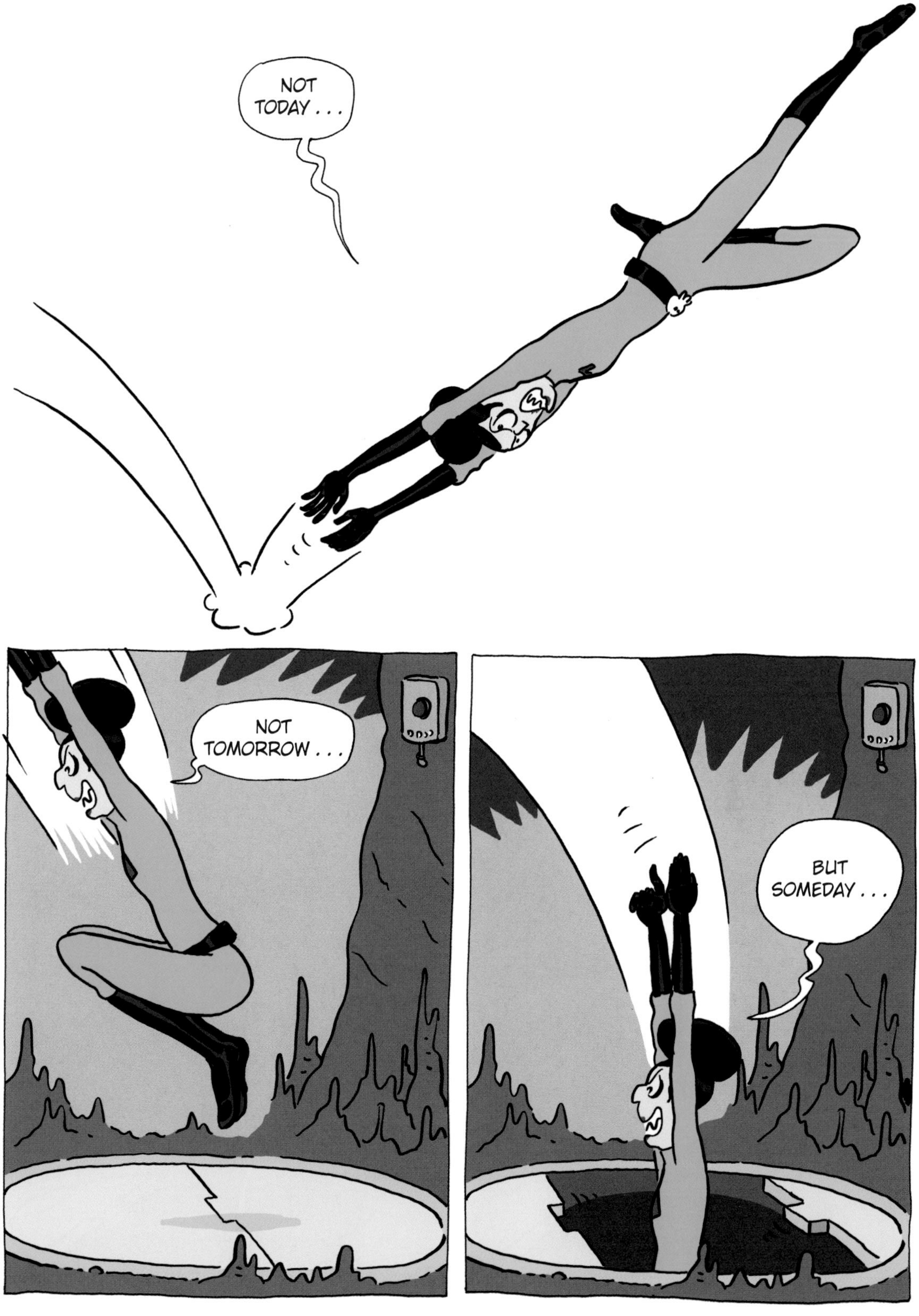
NOT TODAY . . .
NOT TOMORROW . . .
BUT SOMEDAY . . .

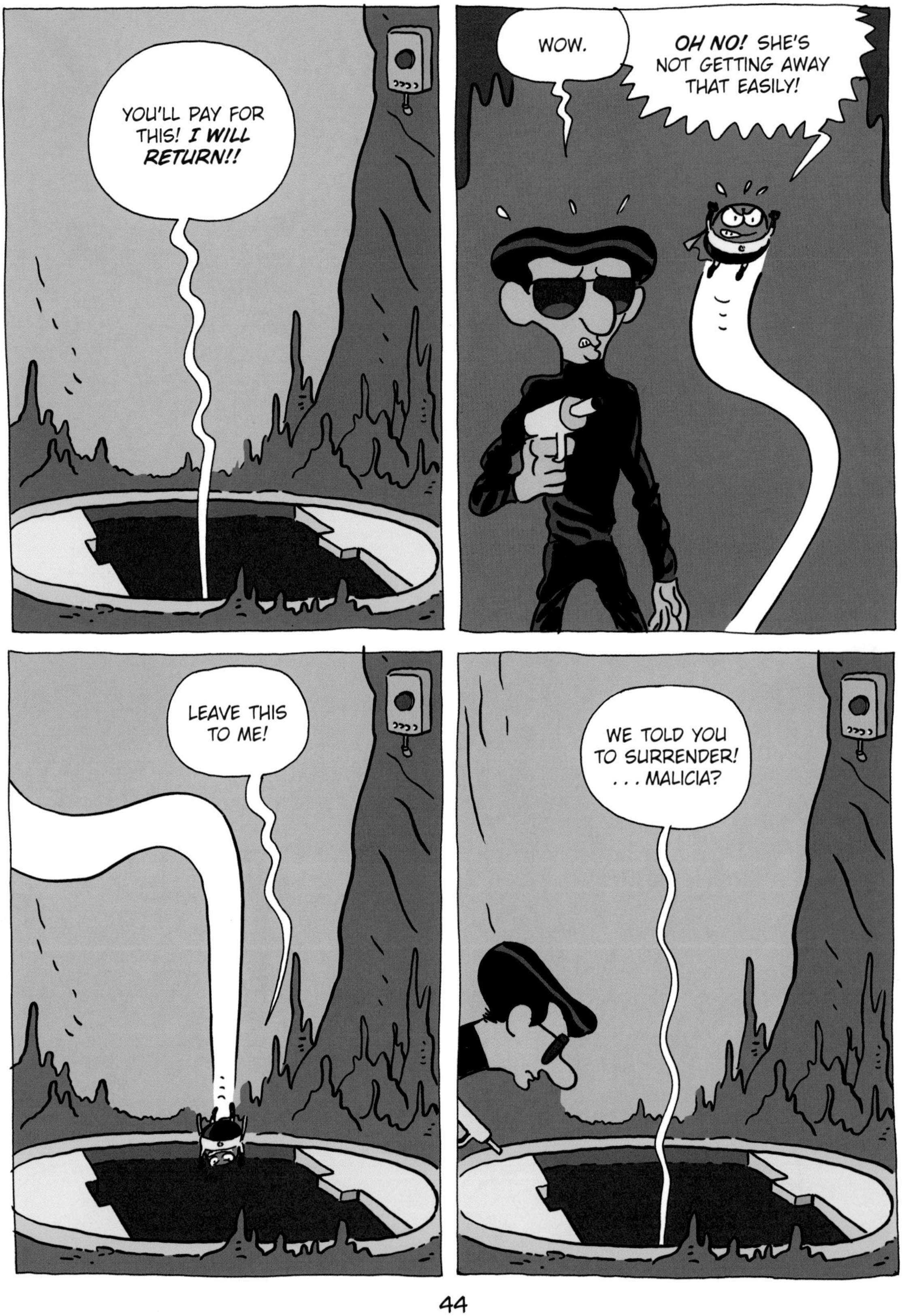
YOU'LL PAY FOR THIS! *I WILL RETURN!!*
WOW.
OH NO! SHE'S NOT GETTING AWAY THAT EASILY!
LEAVE THIS TO ME!
WE TOLD YOU TO SURRENDER! . . . MALICIA?

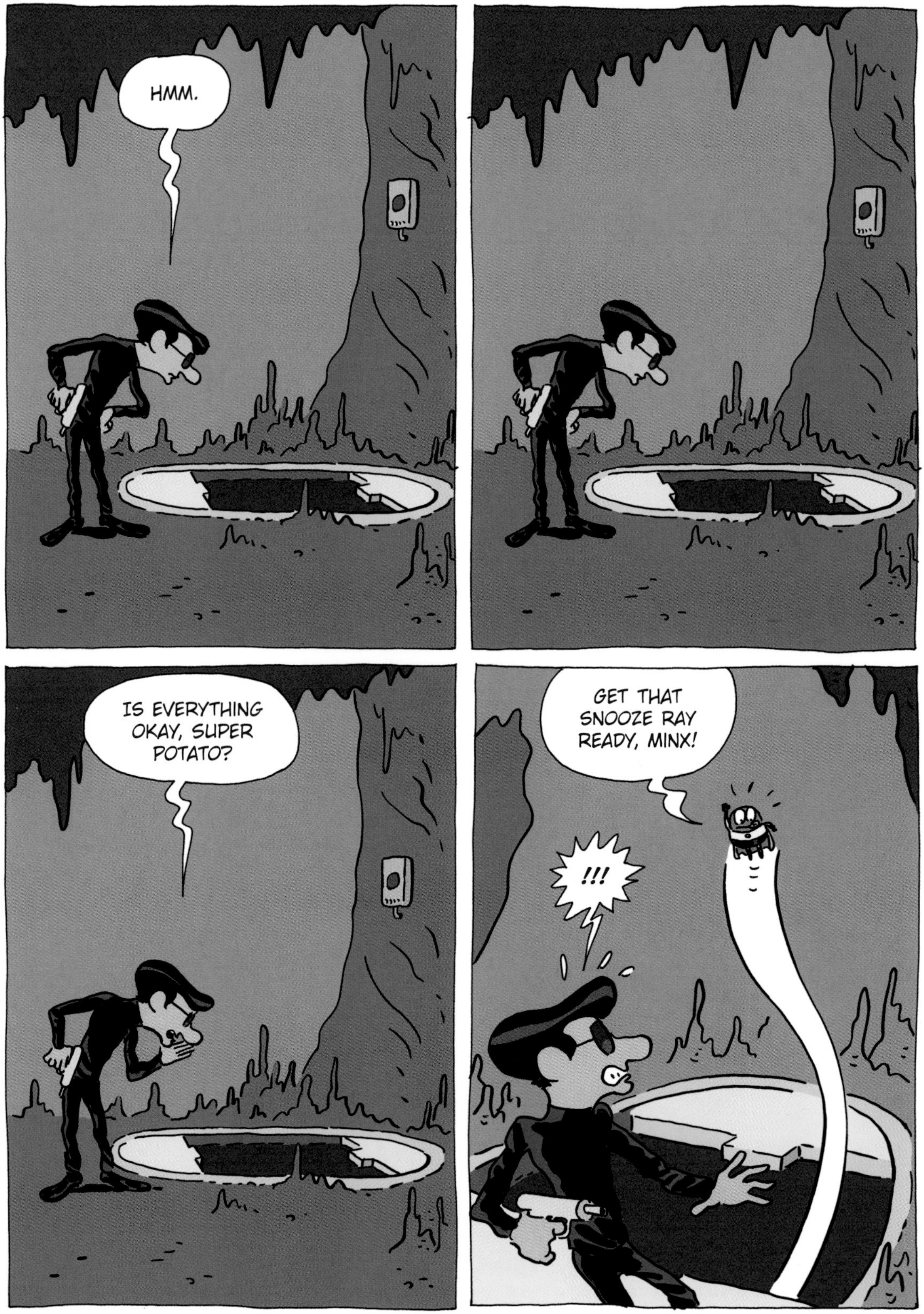
HMM.
IS EVERYTHING OKAY, SUPER POTATO?
GET THAT SNOOZE RAY READY, MINX!
!!!

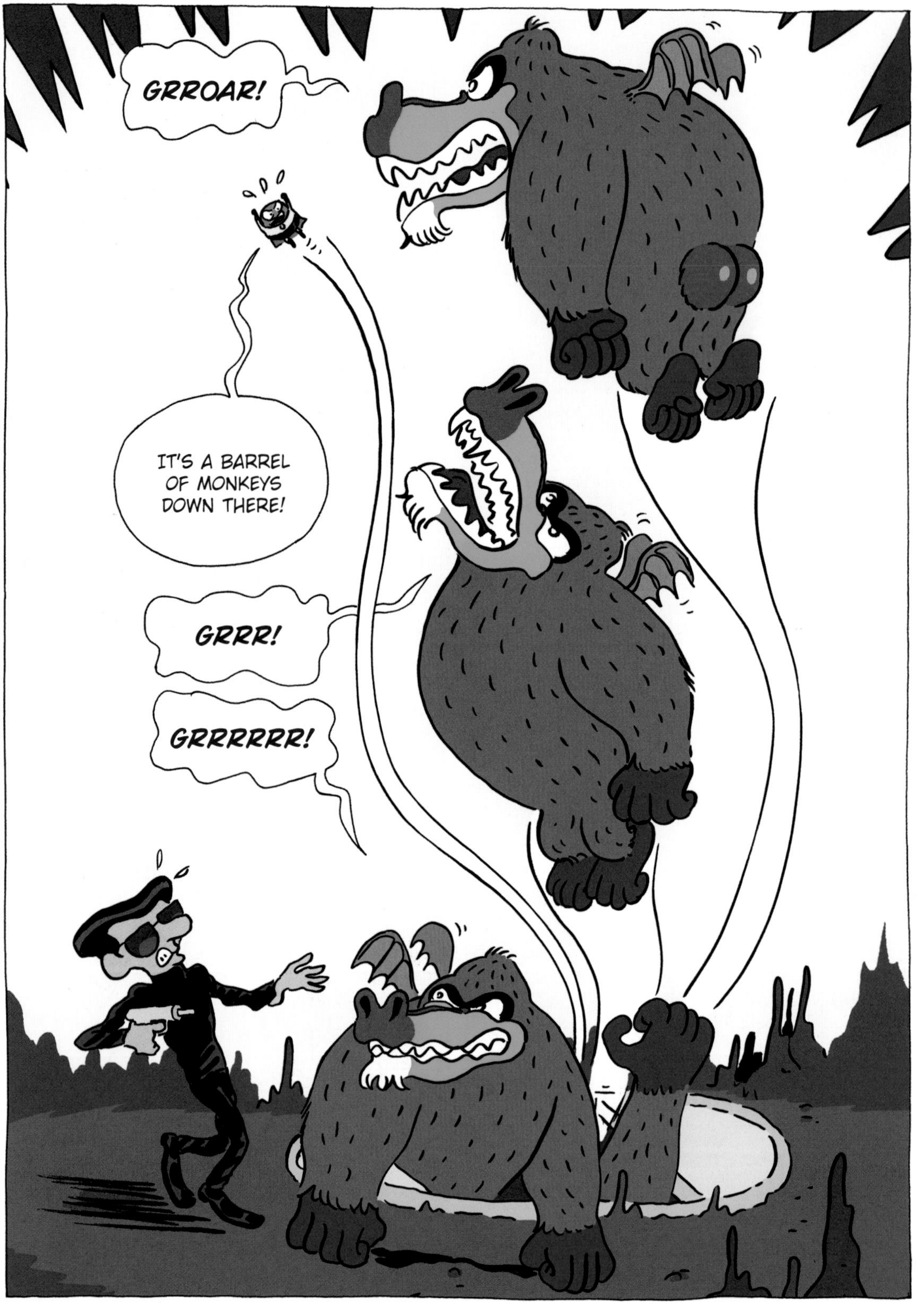
GRROAR!
IT'S A BARREL OF MONKEYS DOWN THERE!
GRRR!
GRRRRRR!

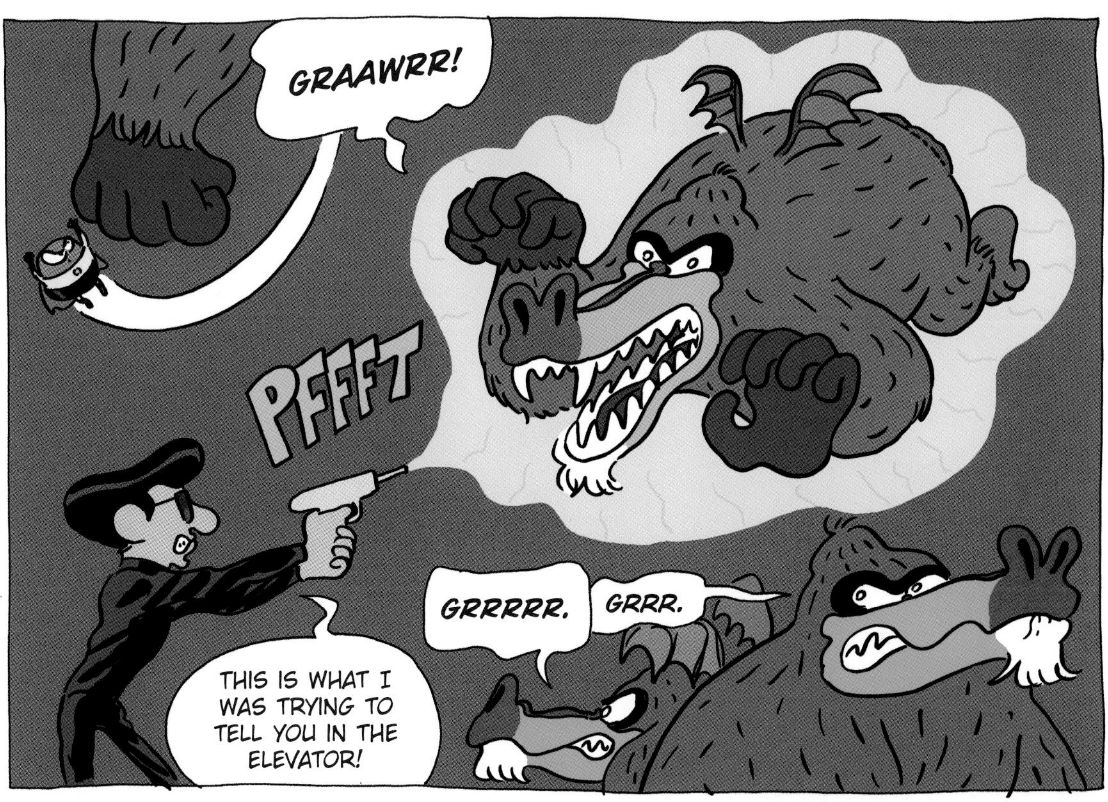
GRAAWRR!
PFFFT
GRRRRR.
GRRR.
THIS IS WHAT I WAS TRYING TO TELL YOU IN THE ELEVATOR!

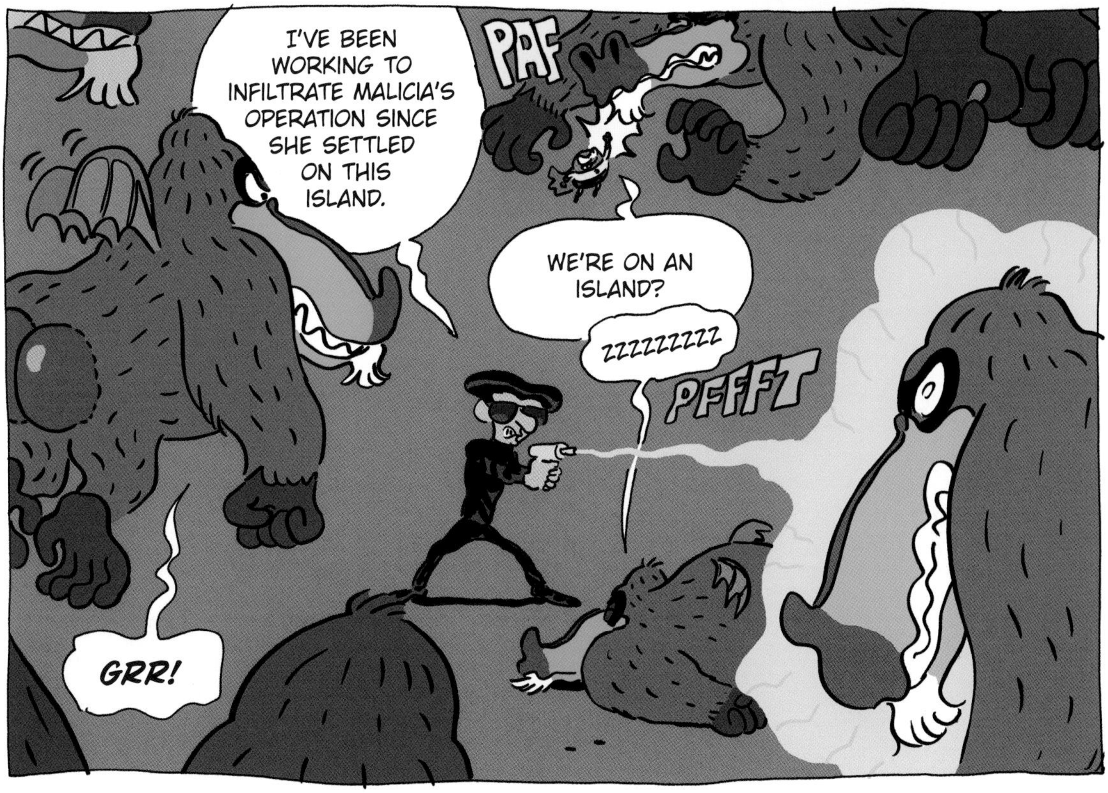
PAF
I'VE BEEN WORKING TO INFILTRATE MALICIA'S OPERATION SINCE SHE SETTLED ON THIS ISLAND.
WE'RE ON AN ISLAND?
ZZZZZZZZZ
PFFFT
GRR!

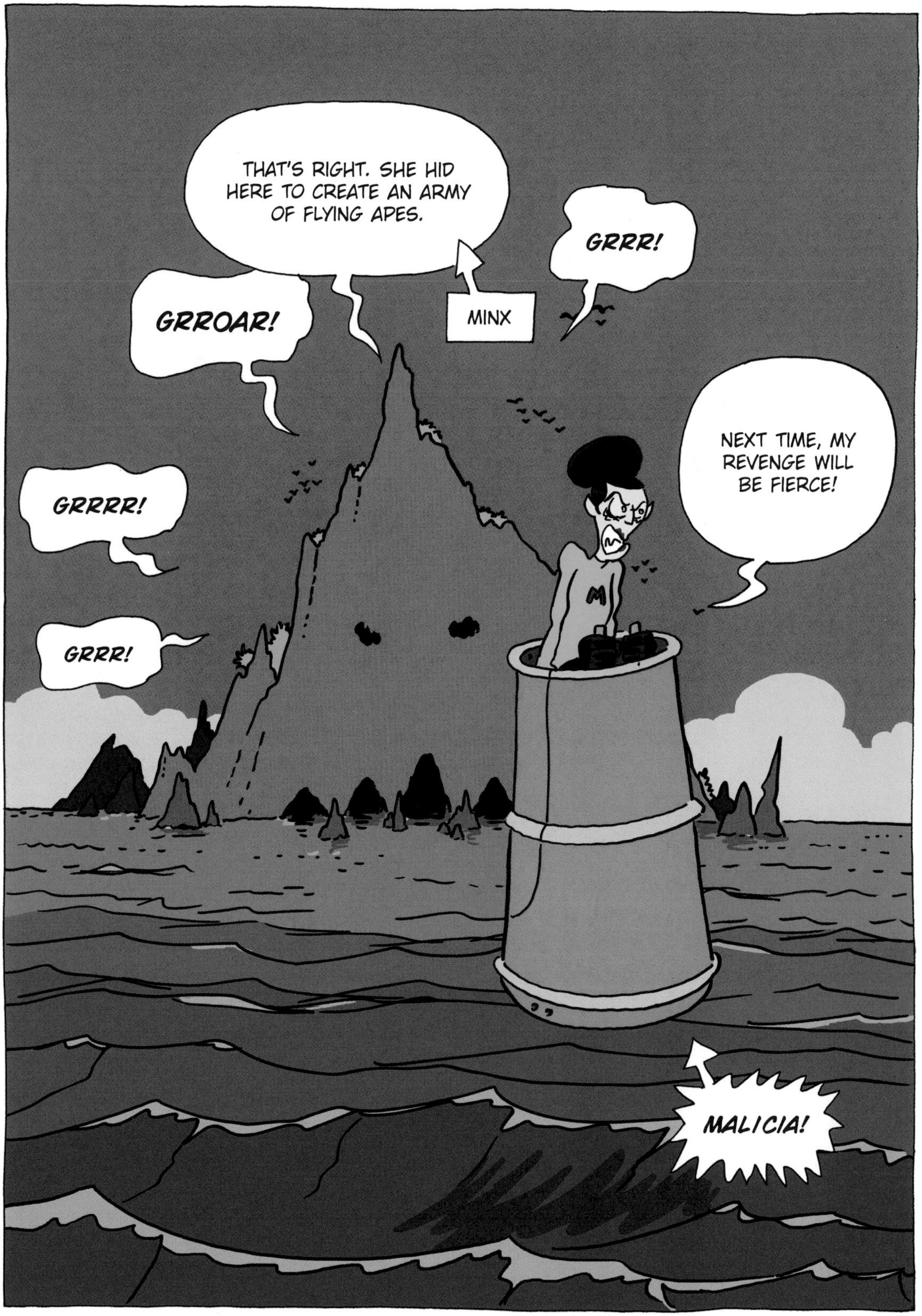
THAT'S RIGHT. SHE HID HERE TO CREATE AN ARMY OF FLYING APES.
MINX
GRRR!
GRROAR!
NEXT TIME, MY REVENGE WILL BE FIERCE!
GRRRR!
GRRR!
MALICIA!

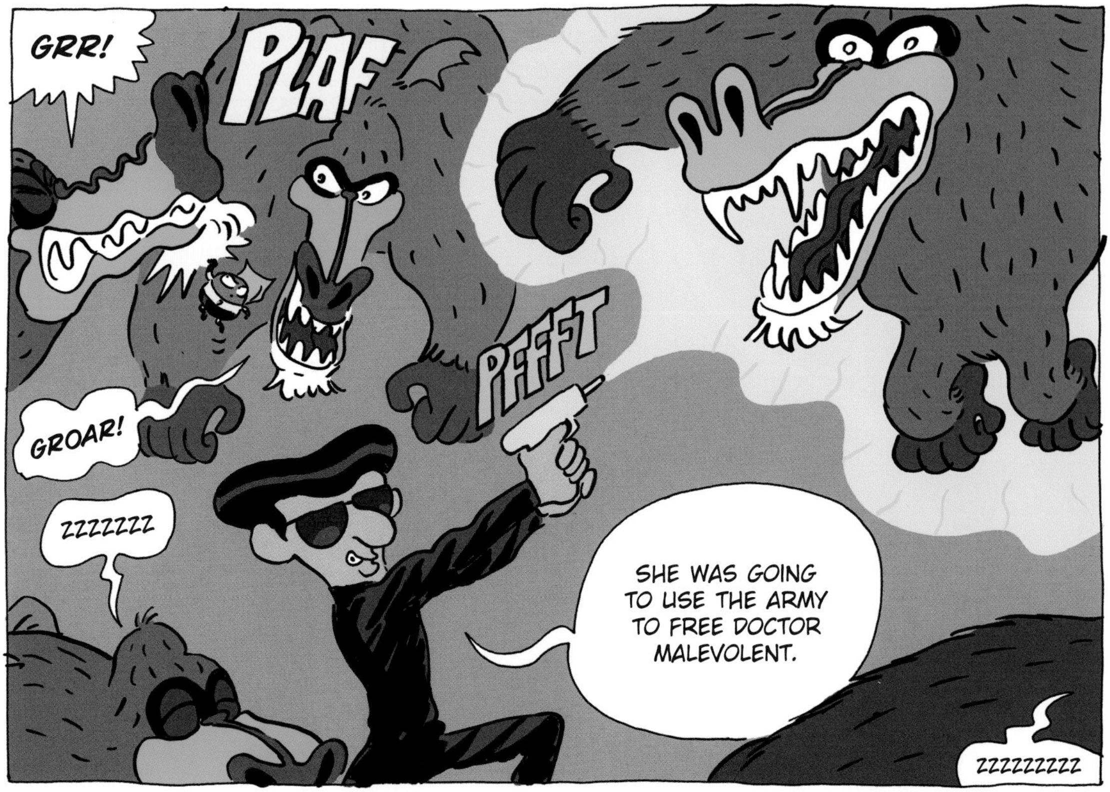
GRR!
PLAF
GROAR!
PFFFT
ZZZZZZZ
SHE WAS GOING TO USE THE ARMY TO FREE DOCTOR MALEVOLENT.
ZZZZZZZZZ

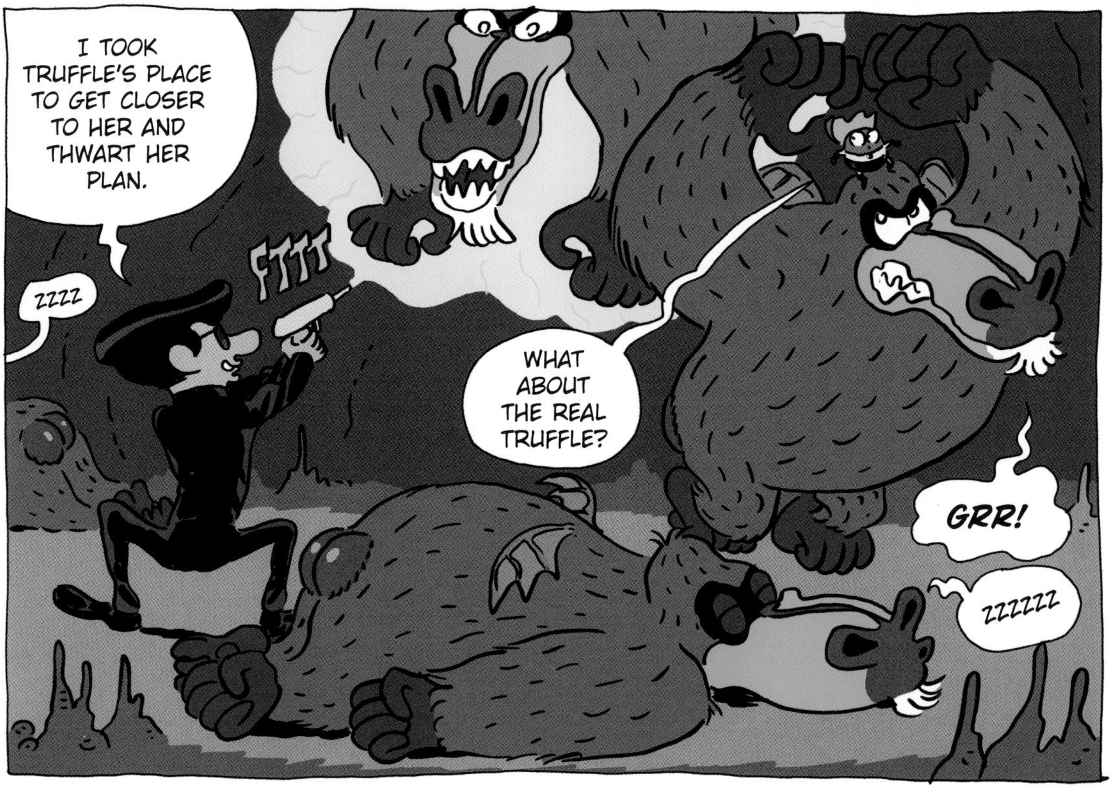
I TOOK TRUFFLE'S PLACE TO GET CLOSER TO HER AND THWART HER PLAN.
ZZZZ
FTTT
WHAT ABOUT THE REAL TRUFFLE?
GRR!
ZZZZZZ

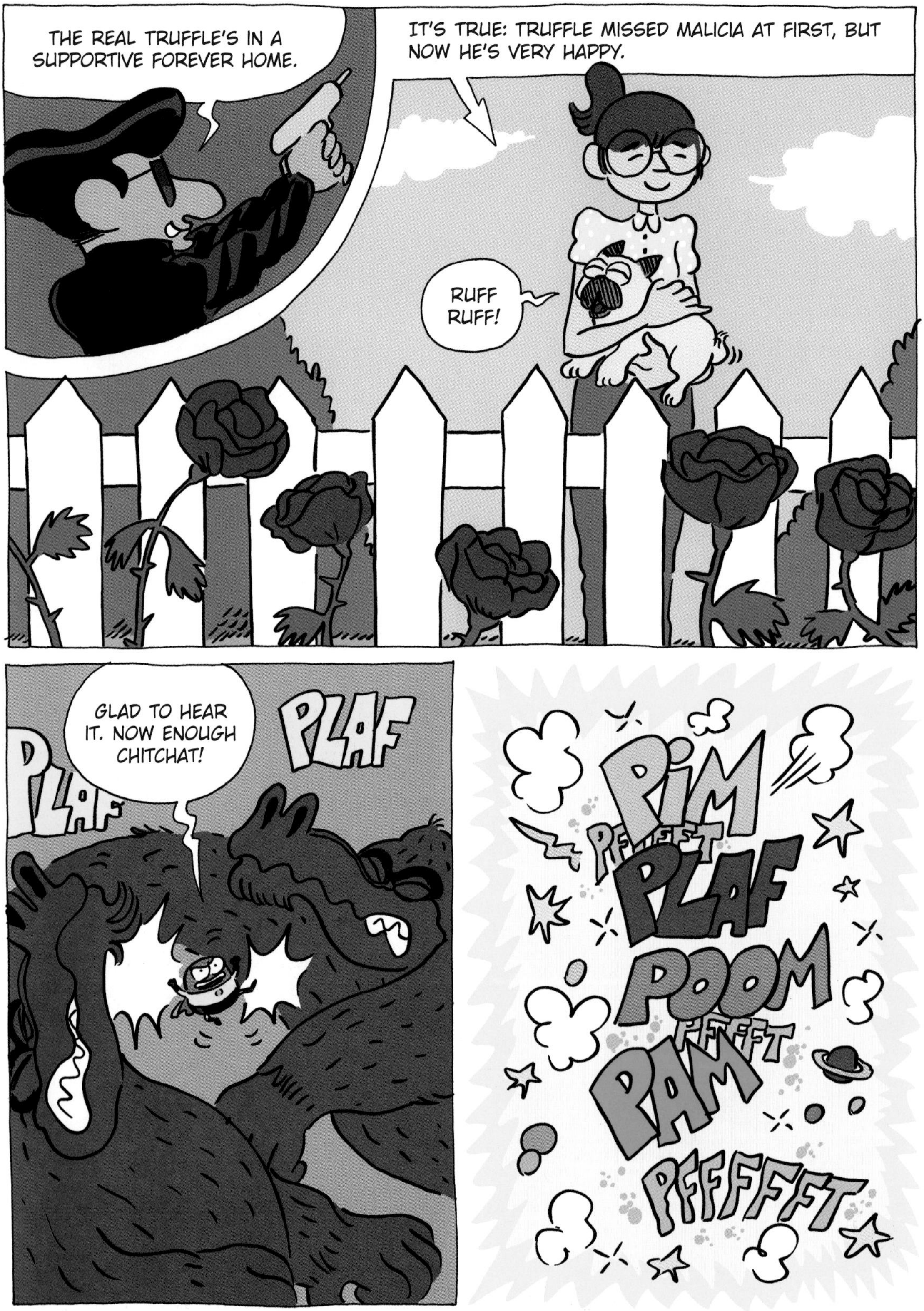
THE REAL TRUFFLE'S IN A SUPPORTIVE FOREVER HOME.
IT'S TRUE: TRUFFLE MISSED MALICIA AT FIRST, BUT NOW HE'S VERY HAPPY.
RUFF RUFF!
GLAD TO HEAR IT. NOW ENOUGH CHITCHAT!
PLAF
PLAF
PIM
PFFFFT
PLAF
POOM
PFFFFT
PAM
PFFFFFFT

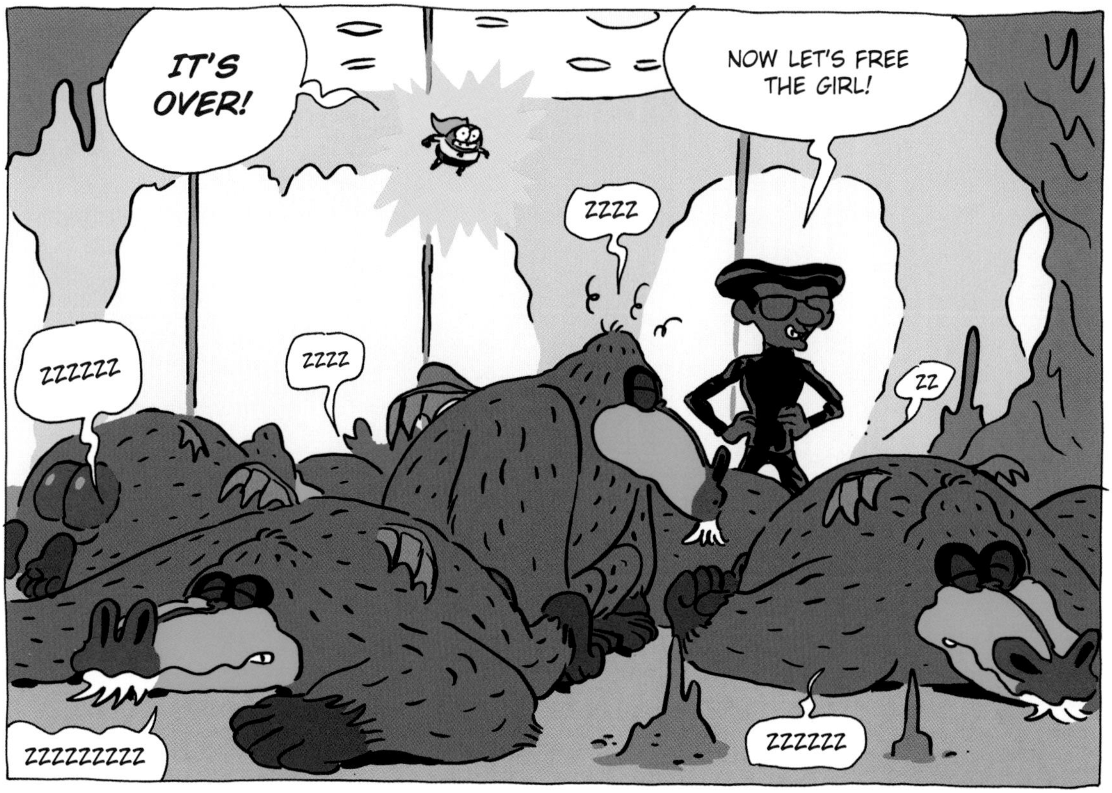
IT'S OVER!
NOW LET'S FREE THE GIRL!
ZZZZ
ZZZZZZ
ZZZZ
ZZ
ZZZZZZZZZ
ZZZZZZ
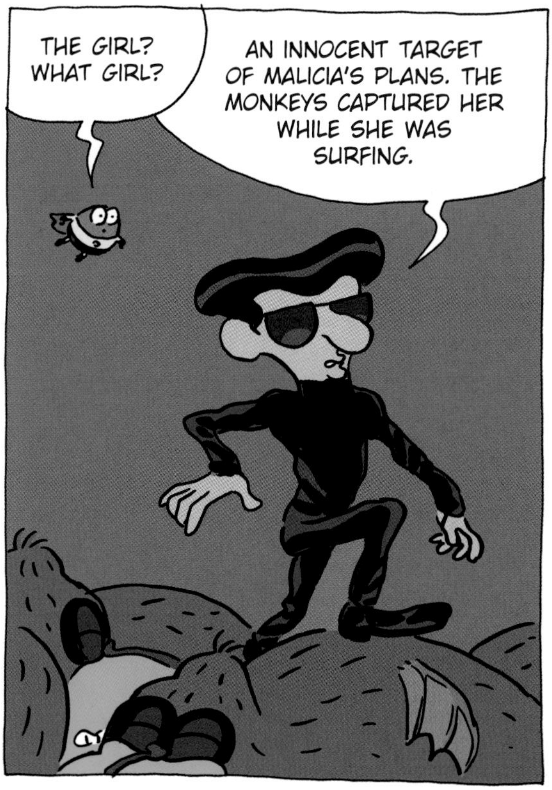
THE GIRL? WHAT GIRL?
AN INNOCENT TARGET OF MALICIA'S PLANS. THE MONKEYS CAPTURED HER WHILE SHE WAS SURFING.
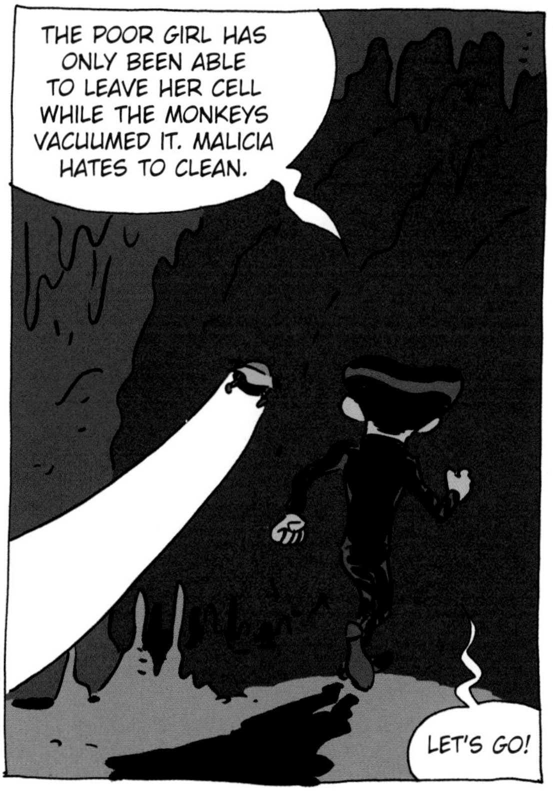
THE POOR GIRL HAS ONLY BEEN ABLE TO LEAVE HER CELL WHILE THE MONKEYS VACUUMED IT. MALICIA HATES TO CLEAN.
LET'S GO!

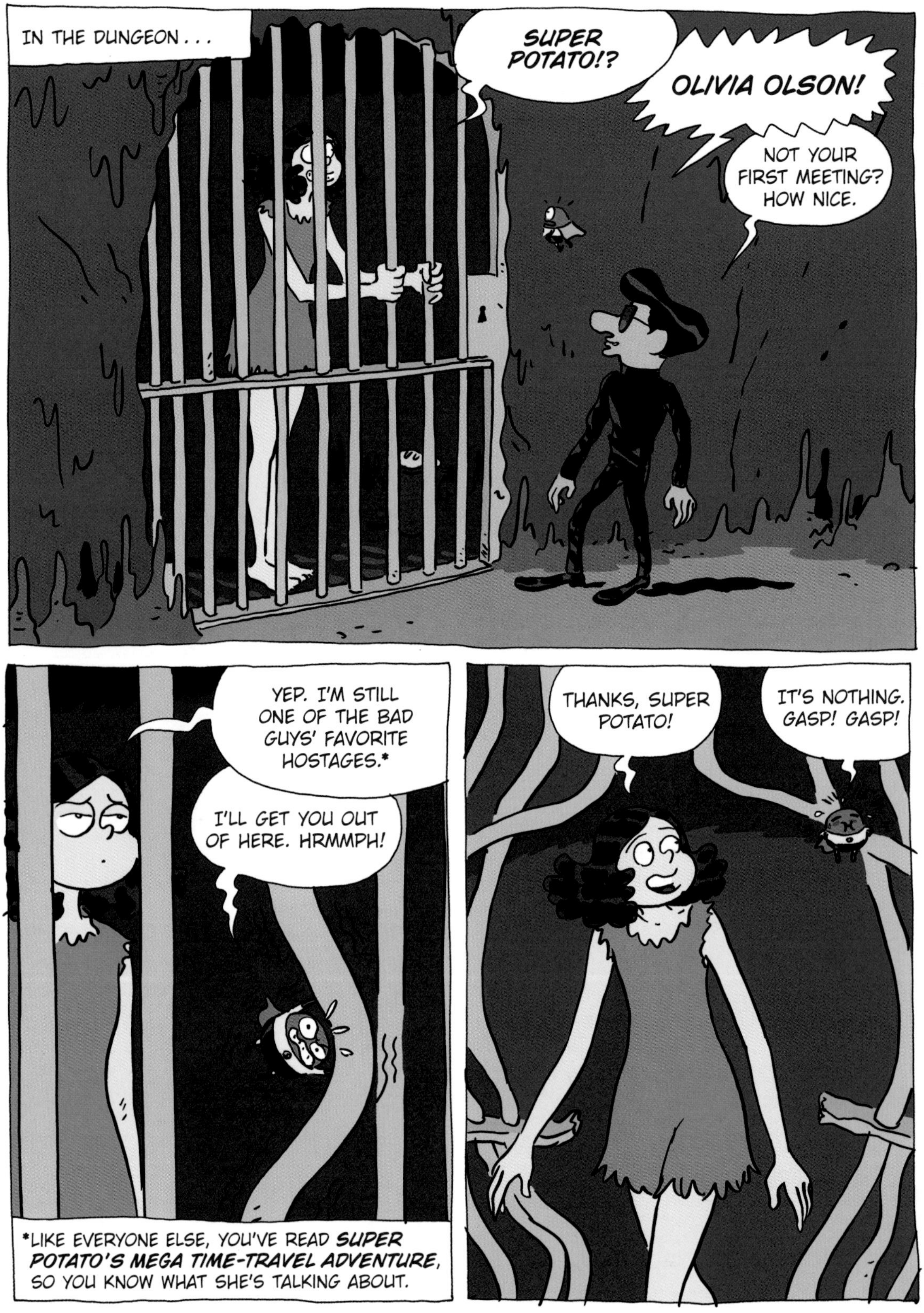
IN THE DUNGEON . . .
SUPER POTATO!?
OLIVIA OLSON!
NOT YOUR FIRST MEETING? HOW NICE.
YEP. I'M STILL ONE OF THE BAD GUYS' FAVORITE HOSTAGES.*
I'LL GET YOU OUT OF HERE. HRMMPH!
*LIKE EVERYONE ELSE, YOU'VE READ **SUPER POTATO'S MEGA TIME-TRAVEL ADVENTURE**, SO YOU KNOW WHAT SHE'S TALKING ABOUT.
THANKS, SUPER POTATO!
IT'S NOTHING. GASP! GASP!

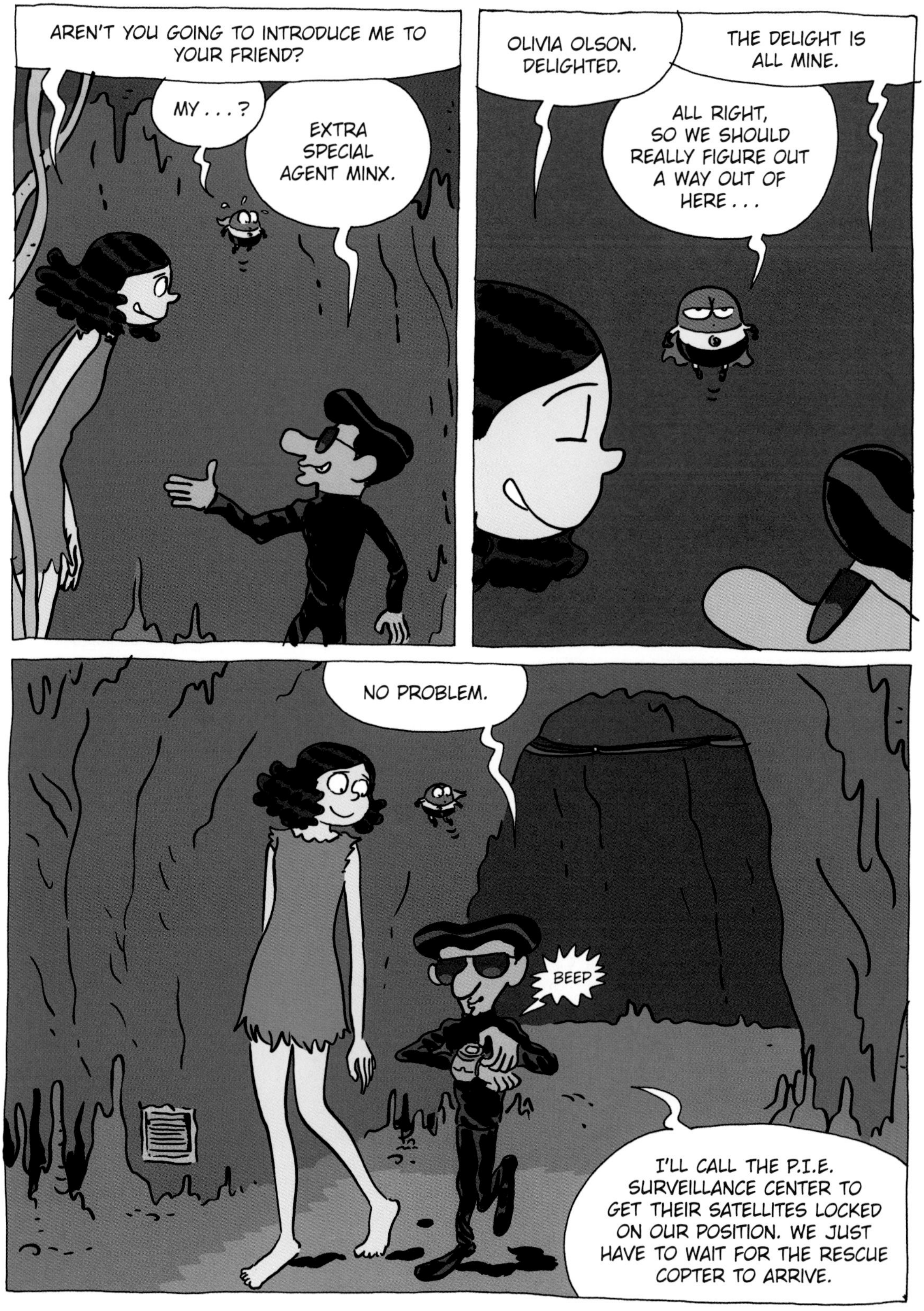
AREN'T YOU GOING TO INTRODUCE ME TO YOUR FRIEND?
MY . . . ?
EXTRA SPECIAL AGENT MINX.
OLIVIA OLSON. DELIGHTED.
THE DELIGHT IS ALL MINE.
ALL RIGHT, SO WE SHOULD REALLY FIGURE OUT A WAY OUT OF HERE . . .
NO PROBLEM.
BEEP
I'LL CALL THE P.I.E. SURVEILLANCE CENTER TO GET THEIR SATELLITES LOCKED ON OUR POSITION. WE JUST HAVE TO WAIT FOR THE RESCUE COPTER TO ARRIVE.

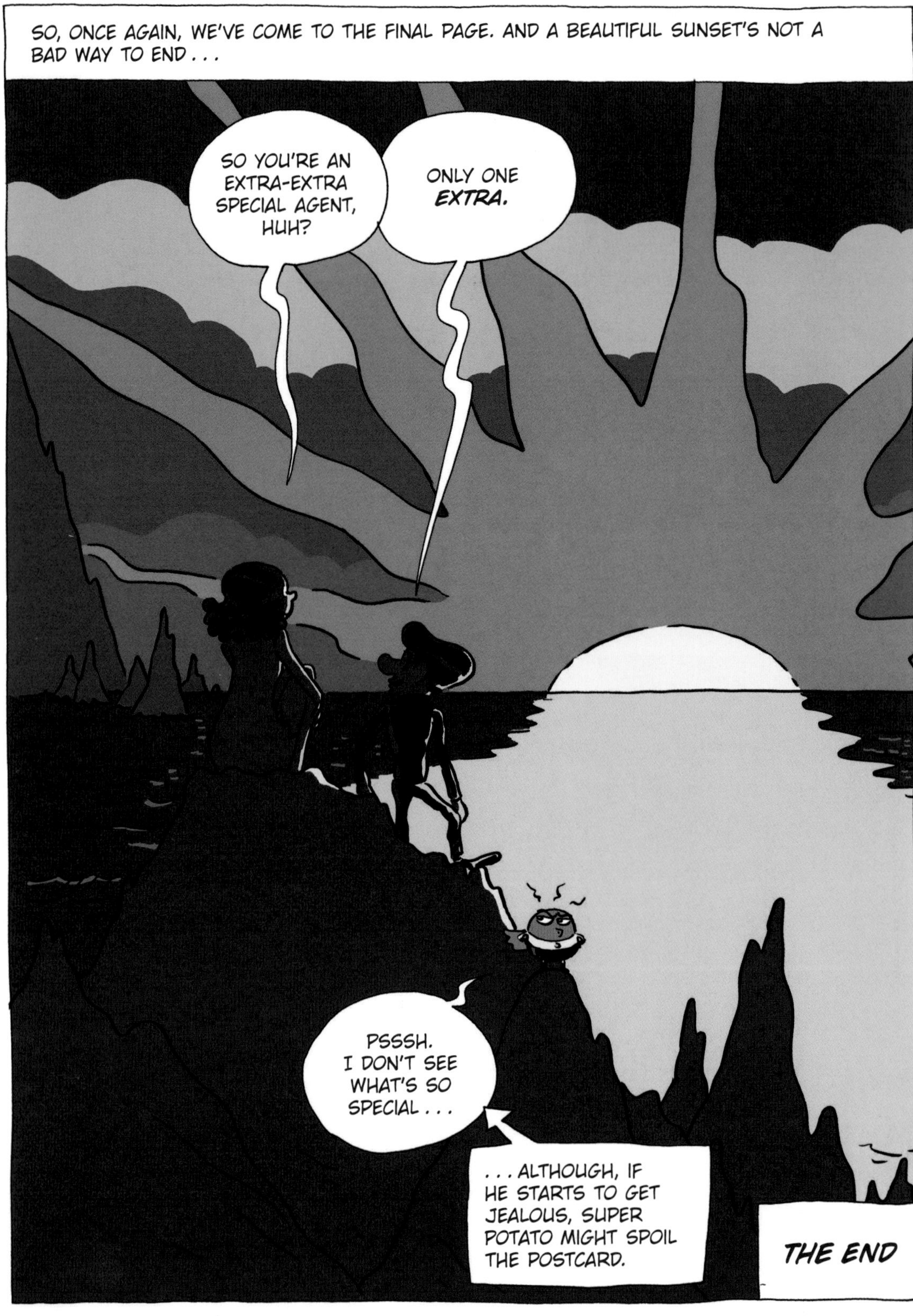
SO, ONCE AGAIN, WE'VE COME TO THE FINAL PAGE. AND A BEAUTIFUL SUNSET'S NOT A BAD WAY TO END . . .
SO YOU'RE AN EXTRA-EXTRA SPECIAL AGENT, HUH?
ONLY ONE *EXTRA.*
PSSSH. I DON'T SEE WHAT'S SO SPECIAL . . .
. . . ALTHOUGH, IF HE STARTS TO GET JEALOUS, SUPER POTATO MIGHT SPOIL THE POSTCARD.
THE END

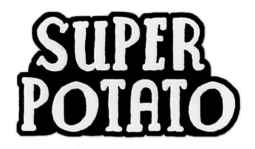

SUPER POTATO

Also available:

**THE EPIC ORIGIN
OF SUPER POTATO**

**SUPER POTATO'S
GALACTIC BREAKOUT**

**SUPER POTATO'S
MEGA TIME-TRAVEL ADVENTURE**

SUPER POTATO
#1 THE EPIC ORIGIN OF SUPER POTATO
Artur Laperla

SUPER POTATO
#2 SUPER POTATO'S GALACTIC BREAKOUT
Artur Laperla

SUPER POTATO
#3 SUPER POTATO'S MEGA TIME-TRAVEL ADVENTURE
Artur Laperla

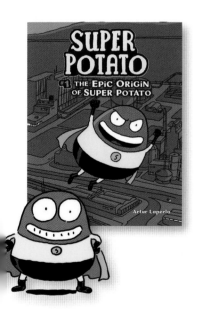

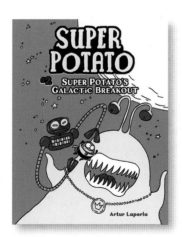

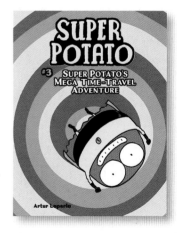

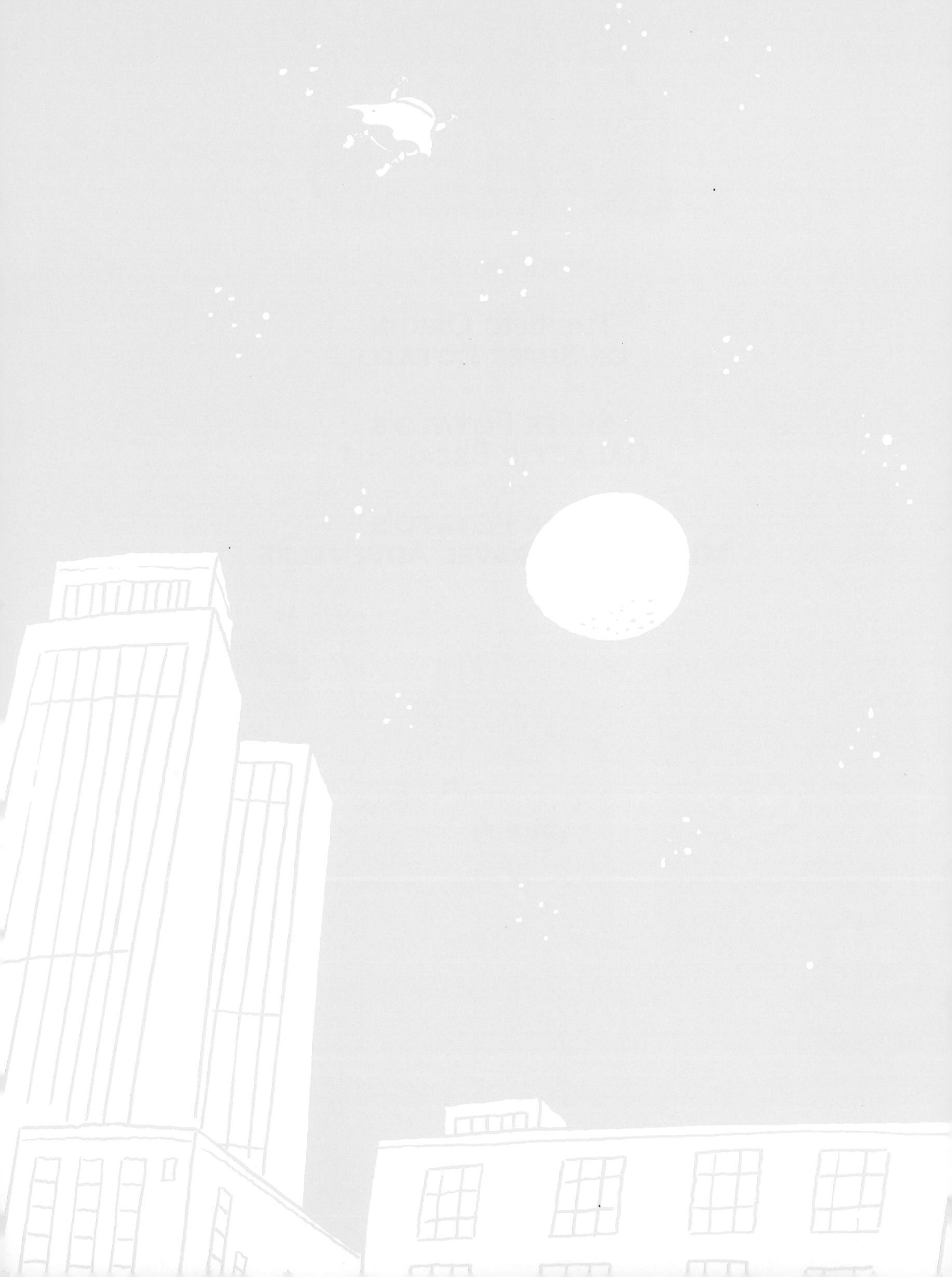